SOVEREIGN BODY

(A NOVEL)

by

Tanure Ojaide

1

Publisher's information, address:
Cissus World Press, P.O. Box 240865, Milwaukee, WI 53224
www.cissusworldpressbooks.com

ISBN: 978-0-967951164
Published in the U.S.A by Cissus World Press

Library of Congress Cataloguing in Publication Data

Ojaide, Tanure

    Sovereign Body
        1. Fiction   II. Nigeria   III. West African Studies
        IV. African/Black Literature   V. Postcolonial Literature

Cover art by Kowho Ojaide.

CISSUS WORLD PRESS BOOKS.

To all the Annies out there

Part I: Annie

1

SMOKE

If I had to marry him because he felt that he already owned me, I wanted to satisfy myself that his purported ownership of my body was false. I was nobody's chattel slave. My heart belonged to me and was nobody else's property to forcibly take away by right of village tradition, however much I respected my parents and uncle who brought the proposal about. My love had to be earned, not taken for granted.

During the five years of his studies abroad, Nathan gave, at best, lukewarm attention to our tradition-sanctioned engagement. During his few visits home, he neither came with fire to me nor got inflamed by my heat. I could fathom neither what scared him in me nor what made him appear so cold to me. We did not even hold hands before he left for Edinburgh. During his first visit home from his overseas studies, I traveled from Yerwa, where I was studying, to visit him, but he turned away when I tried to warm him up with a hug, an embrace, or a kiss. He came to me only when circumstances compelled him to do so when we were stuck together in a room for the night. The river must flow to a lake or the sea! However, his attitude changed somewhat after we both graduated. I had become what he needed to round off his image of a dignified man, a medical doctor, in Barkin Ladi.

It was very much later, after three years of my waiting for him, that he started to curry and gain the favor of some of my people, the most respected in my extended family. It was the educated and the rich who were esteemed and who took decisions on behalf of the others. The family might say that seniority in age mattered, but the poor, who were old, always bowed to the decisions of the few rich. Education brought wealth; education also gave an air of importance to those who had it, and they were highly revered by the people in the village, the core of our family. Those

5

who drove cars and lived in modern houses with shining corrugated iron roofs were not seen as equal with those who might be centenarians but lived in thatched huts and had no other means than their feet for transportation. So, the rich were highly respected because they gave out of their bounty to the poor ones in the family. Those who were perpetual recipients of financial assistance deferred to their benefactors, however young they might be.

I completed my studies more than a year before Nathan Goomsay would qualify as a physician in Edinburgh and then return to Nigeria. After I got a teaching job in Girls' Secondary School, Bukuru, I lived with my maternal uncle, a senior magistrate in the Bukuru Magistrate Court. He had a big five-bedroom mansion to his family, which was very small by our people's standard. My uncle had only a daughter who was away studying at Ahmadu Bello University in the ancient Hausa city of Zaria. I had a big room to myself and that was a great relief in a town where I could not afford a decent accommodation on my own with the poor salary that was the lot of teachers.

The house was built with red bricks and stood imposingly on the hilltop side of town, which the Government had made exclusively the quarters of senior civil servants and white expatriate workers of the nearby tin mines. Built and inhabited by British colonial officers and miners, the houses passed naturally to Nigerian senior staff at independence in 1960. The yard's landscaping was beautiful with the mowed lawns, beautiful cactus and stone hedges, and fine flowers and plants, including whispering pines, eucalyptus, and *neem* trees. The houses in the area were well spaced out and hedges separated them. The quarter stood in stark contrast to other quarters in the town, especially the Tudun Wada and the Angwan Dutse that were not only unplanned but also sprawled without drainage or sewage systems. Bukuru was beautiful and ugly at the same time. I felt fortunate to live with my uncle in the Government Reservation Area, the envy of everyone who did not live there.

My uncle was a disciplined man to the point of rigidity—the kind that one would associate with a robot and not a human being. A tall and fairly robust man, he had a truly magisterial mien. My mother's ancestors, I had been told, had been distinguished hunters often honoured as heroes, and my uncle must have inherited much of the family physique. His hair had grayed early and he did not really need the gray wig that his profession and position demanded he wore over his hair. Many years of legal training and practice might have conditioned him into his present state; if it were not so, I could not see how he derived that aspect of his personality. There was a strict time for everything. A precise time for eating, for bathing, and for brushing teeth; also an exact time for going to bed, among so many other routines. He arranged things in a certain way, and would re-arrange them should his wife or any of us change the very order he had set down. He wanted things done in his own way and loved them only so.

Their daughter, Sarah, studying agricultural economics at Ahmadu Bello University found every possible excuse during breaks and vacations not to come home. So, there was barely anybody other than Rachel and me to mess up the magistrate's ordered life. He refused to have a housemaid, as he expected his wife, Rachel, to take care of him and everything in the house. There were times that he had to re-arrange the cutlery, perhaps in an order he learned during his years in Britain, before taking his dinner. I only looked at him with strange admiration for his meticulous ways and sense of order. At the same time, I pitied him for the manner in which he pursued perfection. This was a man who had to rearrange things that could be ignored before eating, even when he was very hungry. I was not made of that hard or regulated stuff, however much I admired him. Must human beings be gods? Must we not admit some flaws into our dispositions?

I also felt that Magistrate Obida thought that women, including his wife and me, were to be controlled. Women, to him, had to be led; they had to be repeatedly told simple things that men could do without

7

instructions. He repeated things so many times to us that I was often exasperated; but, as my uncle, I had to defer to his orders. At least, to those instructions I did not feel particularly strongly about. What did it matter to me if he told me to bring water in a light green glass and I did so? It was one of a set of glasses that Rachel and I did not like but which he cherished using. He had received the set as a Christmas present the previous year. What did it matter if my uncle asked me to go to bed at ten o'clock when there was a blackout anyway, and I had nothing else to do to keep awake? What did it take away from me if my magistrate uncle asked me to wash his clothes with a specific detergent and I did so with the desired *Omo* type that he gave me money to buy? So, I obeyed him, and it must have pleased him much that I did not question his orders. His wife had for long resigned herself to hearing commands from her magisterial lord.

This man of the law would at home, as in court, brook no open dissent, but we flouted his rules even in the obedience he thought he received from us willy-nilly. How many times had we failed to do what he asked us to do that we felt was too demanding or demeaning? Call it civil disobedience or passive resistance; we knew what we were doing. If somebody took you for a slave, you would have to resist as best you could. Or if he took you for a child, that you were definitely not, you would respond accordingly. Not that we were slaves or children in the real sense. His wife and I knew what would enervate the disciplined man that he thought he was by doing small things we rightly predicted would cross him—making his bath water a little too hot or cold, placing his right and left slippers beside each other in the wrong order. Since he often added salt to his soup before tasting it, we began to spice with more salt than necessary his particular share of food, which we placed on the table for him. We ate separately.

From him, I learnt that even brilliant bossy men had a blind spot in their watch. After all, neat as he tried to look, he cut his finger and toenails regularly, but one of the toenails was naturally defective. I saw it when he stretched his legs from the sofa that he usually sat in. Nobody else sat in that sofa that was reserved for his relaxation at home. So he was not perfect in every way, however much he tried to organize himself at home and perhaps in court. His wife, who washed his underwear, would have known for long that he was not as immaculate as he thought or felt. He attracted dirt like everybody else in Bukuru or, for that matter, on earth. The house was not a magistrate court, and there ought to be a difference between a judge and a family man that was a husband, a father, and an uncle.

I had asked my friend to visit me a week prior to my marriage. It was not an easy decision for me to write and ask him to come and see me. I agonized over what to do. Though the marriage date had been set by my uncle and Nathan and approved by my parents, I had strange feelings about it. The feeling of strangeness increased as the time drew close. After being engaged for more than five years, why should my heart beat awkwardly at the crucial time? Was I going to be entombed in a patriarchy as I saw my uncle's wife live? I kept the letter to Jo for several days, after which I went to the post office to mail it. I joined the line and bought the necessary stamp. However, as I opened the mailbox to drop the letter, I had second thoughts as to whether it was the right thing to do or not. I went back home with the stamped envelope. Later, after two days of pros and cons immobilizing my mind, like one under a spell I went to drop it.

Though I lived with my uncle and his wife, I felt lonely. My friends Debra and Josephine must have surmised that since I was about to marry, they should give me space to relish the special time. But they knew not that neither Nathan nor I were head over heels for the other. What I was doing might not be right, as far as our customs were concerned, but must I die of heat without the person I had come to love dousing the flames and saving me? Must I die in silence or cry out for relief? I chose the course of immediate relief and invited Jo to spend two to three days with me in Bukuru.

So Jo came to town and stayed with his friend who was an accountant in one of the tin-mining companies around. I called him Jo, for short. I had told him that Jonah, his miracle name from the Bible, was too old-fashioned to be called in full. He even once confessed to me that he was not worthy to be called such a holy name. And except for those who knew him from childhood, who sometimes called him the full name, Jo became his only name.

I knew that he would come as I had asked him to in my letter. He would know that I needed him badly to invite him from Lagos at that crucial time. After his year of sabbatical leave at the University of Yerwa, he had gone back to the University of Lagos, his home institution. During the afternoon of his arrival, I went with Josephine, my girlfriend, to see him at his friend's, 7A Amo Street. We had lived in the town for two years, but we still expected difficulty in locating the place. In the Tudun Wada quarter, street names and numbers were erratic and generally difficult to locate, but we were lucky that the first motorcyclist we asked for direction pointed out the street to us. Once in the street, we easily found the compound that was boldly numbered. It stood out from most of the other compounds around.

As usual, whenever we met, Jo lit up when he saw me and I shook with tenderness when we hugged. He wore no perfumes that I could think of, nor any body cream of designer type. However, I felt like not letting go of him. I was already used to his familiar aroma of freshness that I had always enjoyed experiencing. We exchanged a few pleasantries as the presence of both his friend and mine would allow in such circumstances. I promised him that I would be back later that evening. I wanted him to taste again the fruit that could be either soured or robbed from me by Dr. Nathan Goomsay. I had to relish what I enjoyed while it lasted before it changed to a different taste I could not imagine.

My uncle's wife, Rachel, noticed how changed I was when I got home. I was embarrassed and could not remain calm as I prepared to go back to Jo. I was shivering with tenderness. Like a plant obeying the wind, I moved where thoughts of him carried me. And that was far.

My uncle's wife must have observed my distractions as I handed her a tablespoon when she asked for pepper. I had been transported so far away in thought that I did not hear what she asked me to bring at close quarters. I nodded to what she said but did not really understand because my imagination had taken flight. I hurried to the bathroom to look at myself in the mirror. I was feeling warm, but there were no sweat beads on my face. I tripped as I crossed back to the kitchen through the sitting room. How could I not see the stool before the mortar and pestle? Once in a while, instead of standing, Rachel or I sat to pound yam or millet with the big pestle. Rachel gazed at me, dipping a ladle into the soup pot to taste it.

"Are you all right?" she asked.

I normally assisted her in preparing dinner in the kitchen. Both of us talked more intimately in the kitchen, which the magistrate did not enter. He always asked for what he wanted from the kitchen to be brought to him, and Rachel and I enjoyed having our occasional women's talk without interference.

"Yes, I am. But why do you ask me whether I am all right or not?" I asked back. "Nothing," she said.

There is a way of saying "Nothing" that you know there must be something kept back. I knew she was fully aware of what I was going through. Many women must go through it perhaps, this fear of what marriage could bring. Would it be a burdensome yoke or an interesting partnership? Was she thinking I had gone to meet Nathan and was excited by the aftertaste? She knew I was restless due to something, but I did not think she could really tell its source.

I foresaw a battle of wills ahead that night, and I would need Rachel on my side. I told her that I was going to spend the night with my girlfriends at Josephine's. Of course, she knew them.

"I don't think so," she said, "with your face flushed with emotions that I can't describe? You have changed from your normal looks. You bristle with excitement—it is all over you, your face, eyes, your whole body brimming over with excitement. You must love him so much to be so excited. You must be lucky."

I was at a loss of what she was talking about. Who was the man, the "him"? Did she know that I was going to another man? She must have known that I was not going to tell lies to go to Dr. Nathan Goomsay's in Barkin Ladi more than thirty kilometers away. Why would you steal what had already been apportioned to you, even if by a formula that you did not understand? Somehow, we women intuitively feel for each other in a situation like this. I believe that that night my uncle's wife knew I was going out for somebody or something else that I was ready to die for, and that it could not be Dr. Goomsay to whom my family had me yoked.

"You must tell your uncle that you are going to your girlfriends who are holding a party for you, and that you'll be back in the morning. If he insists that you must come back late, tell him you will; but do what pleases you," she counseled.

Rachel and I became friends and fellow conspirators. She understood my feelings, how deep and turbulent like a river's currents on a sloping terrain they were. In her early forties, she had been married for more than twenty years. She had not seen her future husband before she was betrothed to him. My uncle had gone to study Law in London and when he was about to come back from studies abroad, it was deemed necessary to have a wife waiting for him at home. Rachel was young and very pretty. Many suitors were already coming to her parents. On the verge of coming out of secondary school, she was very excited about the prospects of marrying a lawyer and accepted who was proposed to her—a

12

lawyer educated in London! She had told me many times how her husband did not treat her like a man who had been in England should, from the stories she read about English people and love. I was afraid I could be trapped in a similar way. Respect for one's customs must not be too total as not to loosen or cut the stifling rope it holds for you.

As our people say, you don't have to be a farmer to recognize yam's leaves, if you see them. I rightly foresaw my uncle's response. I waited till he sat on his sofa in the sitting room, legs stretched leisurely, and reading the day's newspapers he had no time to read in the office. Once in a while he took a bottle of Rock beer that he mixed with *Fanta* orange, and he seemed to relish it. He was sipping the cocktail from his favorite tall light green glass with a straw and I thought that moment of relaxation was best for me to tell him my plan for the night.

"You are getting married next week. Why do you have to go out? No, no, no; you can't go out," he over-ruled.

It seemed too that he knew that I was not really going to a party organized by my friends; nor was I going at night to Nathan in Barkin Ladi. I believe he sensed my heart beating loud for something he was not familiar with; something he suspected was burning in me that he was too timid to assist me to douse. Love smells more than perfumes, our people say. I saw in him some confusion; moved by my appeal and yet his manly duty, as he saw it, to foreclose any way that would make me deviate from fidelity to my proposed husband. I did not blame him because, from his close friendship with Nathan, he would not be an accessory to my cheating on him just a week before the marriage he enthusiastically approved. He could not enter my woman's mind though and so could not relieve me of my heart's fire.

"No, no, no," he shouted again at me, as if to shake off a lenient inclination about to take control of him.

A fly flew past his drinking glass, which he took from the side table and held up as if to propose a toast. He placed it back on the table after

13

assuring himself that the fly had gone away. He took away the straw from the glass, gulped the drink, coughed as if choked for a half-minute, and went into his bedroom to meet his wife who was making their bed. He offered me no opportunity to contradict his order. The magistrate had spoken and the court rose!

Despite my guardian's refusal for me to spend the night out, I knew no matter what happened that I must go to meet Jo. I had no doubts in my mind that I would meet him, even if afterward I would have to be marched through the streets of Bukuru as a prostitute for men to pour insults upon. I had seen such incidents in the village and in town, but fear of humiliation would not deter me a bit. Except God, nobody could stop me on this. I was hell-bent on having my desire however others, especially relatives, might perceive my action. It was time for me to seize what I wanted, no matter the consequence. In this case, if I were refused marriage, it would be great relief. I was so confused about everything, including the marriage and my invitation to Jo to visit from Lagos, but now I had to meet him.

What had I not gone through before, for the sake of Dr. Jonah Ogbe? So much had happened in the five years since the engagement ceremony at home. Only six months ago, I had been summoned to a family council in Nang to be shamed by the man who wanted me to marry him. The details of that incident always enrage me. This time, even if Nathan knew, I did not expect any worse repercussion. I thought of myself as smoke. Our young women were not allowed to have praise-names, but already I saw myself as Smoke, she who cannot be contained.

My mother had told me how, as a young woman, she used to be prevented from seeing my father. She would arrange to see him on a market day when both of them met and talked to their hearts' content. Yes, the market was their cover, she told me. No matter how hard her parents tried to keep her away from her lover, she found a way to see him. She composed a song about him, which she sang while with her female playmates on moonlit nights. The song possessed her, and she knew that her girlfriends knew what she was going through in love. Up till now, I find it difficult to believe that she went through such lengths to see my father. From the way they now lived, one could barely imagine how they could have been such young lovers. It could be that the fire had long gone out of their relationship.

I was prepared to go to any lengths to meet Jo that night. I was ready for any ordeal, flagellation, torture, or humiliation after I gave him the fruit that I wanted both of us to share in secret communion. Short of being shackled to a rock with a chain I couldn't break, I was going to free myself to go where I had to be that night.

Ten o'clock passed. I sat reading in the dining room that adjoined the sitting room. Of course, my mind was not in the book I was reading. What was I reading *Macbeth* for when I had no examination to write? I was not teaching the book either. I just wanted to wear my uncle out in his waiting game. Finally at eleven my uncle and his wife went to bed; later than usual because they were watching me. I had become a suspect who had to be guarded. Poor aunt Rachel was an unwilling guard. At some stage she had winked her eyes mischievously, as if to say they knew what I was going out for. Before Uncle Solomon went into his room, he reminded me,

"Annie, you must not go out. It is my order."

At other times I would have considered the consequences of flouting his magisterial order. Tonight, his order would not stop me from the tryst. I waited another fifteen minutes or so, when I felt he should fall asleep after assuring himself that I would do his bidding. And so I opened the door and ran out. I thought I heard my uncle asking who was opening the door, but I left, driven to whom my heart was pounding fast and hard. I was not myself. I appeared possessed by some spirit that would lead me safe through any imaginable dangers in the streets of Bukuru. God, forgive me!

How I got to Jo that night continues to haunt my memory. The streets were already almost empty. Unlike the past few days when there was no electric light, there was light this time. I did not know whether it was a blessing or a curse. If I was in the dark, nobody would see me—but I would be prone to danger. In the light, my guardian uncle could drive after me and make a fool of both of us. The taxi drivers had gone for the night. In haste, I had forgotten to go into my bedroom to take money to pay for my taxi fare. So it would have been useless if the taxi drivers were still working. I knew I had a long trek to make, and that would take me far into the night.

It was cool, the breeze gentle. In mid-March the afternoon rains that brought cold had not come. The harmattan left with its frosty cold in mid-February. I pulled off my rubber slippers and held them, after the strap of one of them snapped off. I knew I had to half-jog, half-walk to get to my forbidden destination before it was too late. The tall trees that lined the streets cast their shadows on the road. Dogs barked from walled compounds. Some birds flew past—I had thought birds should be ensconced in their nests and sleeping at that late hour.

Tudun Wada streets were not lit, unlike those in the Government Reservation Area. I did not care whether monsters stalked me in the dark; I wanted to get to Jo as soon as I could. I prayed that the gate to the compound would not be shut and thus make it difficult to get in. A car's light flashed at me from afar but the vehicle passed without stopping. I would not have asked for a ride from a stranger anyway, so late at night. Fortunately, my uncle had not pursued me like a lost dog or cat that had to be leashed and taken back home.

I thought about what I was doing. It might not be right, but could I help it? I was already on the way and some inexorable force was pulling me along. I covered the eight kilometers or so that separated me from Jo, forgetful of time.

Jo told me what transpired on his side as he waited for me that night. I told him that he would have so disappointed me if he wavered in his feelings for me. I would have concluded that men were not reliable. Thanks to his love and confidence in me, he did not heed his friend's reckless advice.

William Efe was a senior accountant at the New Nigeria Mining Company, the main rival of Amalgamated Tin Mines of Nigeria. The two companies were the most dominant in the mining industry in the area. William lived in what most people would call the livable part of Tudun Wada quarter of Bukuru. His walled compound had two three-apartment houses, one of which he rented. He was jovial and light-hearted. I did not know much about him till later. When Jo told him about me, Mr. Efe did not understand the depth of our relationship, complex as it was. It was difficult for anybody else to understand our bond. So his carefree response to Jo's anxiety about me was not surprising, more so as many female university students had created an irresponsible lifestyle around there. The female residential area of the campus was like a market from dusk to dawn.

As early as seven in the evening, William had doubted that I would come as I had promised Jo.

"Come on, Jo, go and take one of the university girls out. There are many and any will follow you for the asking," he said.

It was shameful that the university halls of residence had turned to glamorized brothels, I ruminated.

"No, I don't take girls just for the asking. In any case, Annie will definitely come, unless she can't help it and it will take a lot to stop her. I know she will risk her life to come to me. She invited me here from Lagos and she already came this afternoon to give her word to be with me this night. I know she won't fail," he told him.

"Trust a young woman to that extent?" he asked.

"Why not? I trust her entirely."

After nine o'clock had passed and I had not arrived, as Jo told me later, William started to ridicule him. The mockery intensified with every passing half-hour.

"You could have had a beautiful student to sleep with," he said as if regretting Jo's self-inflicted folly.

He even said that Jo put all his eggs in one basket, and in the event of an accident he would lose all.

Jo told me: "I felt hurt by his jibes. I didn't like the lighthearted way he talked about laying with girls, as if they were commodities in the street market. I tried to explain how I felt about you, but his conception of a relationship between a man and a woman was very shallow indeed. He did not understand what love meant, and had not come close to experiencing it, I believe, from his reckless jokes. He made me laugh in spite of myself when I said that even if I had to talk with you all night, our bodies swathed in one sheet, I would feel fulfilled.

"Bring a woman to talk all night!" he cried in disbelief, indicating my weird proposition.

Jo was more than doubly sure that I would come to him. And that gladdened my heart—his total confidence in me, the trust without which there could be no meaningful relationship. And, of course, I did arrive. Fortunately, the gate was not locked, perhaps in anticipation of my arrival. At 12:35 a.m. I knocked at the apartment door. Jo must have jumped from his bed, all along his ears anxious for my knock. He let me in, then went back to lock the gate. I was breathing fast.

He came back in a moment and held my hand and led me into his room, spare but cozy—only one chair and a writing table. Hanging on the white-painted wall was the New Nigeria Mining Company's official calendar. We sat on the low bed. His friend must have long fallen asleep dreaming of Jo's missed opportunities.

That night consolidated the stars that would continue to shine in our firmament. That night sowed the seeds of the berry that would always

18

be ours alone to share. The pact of that night ensured me a constant companion on a solitary road for decades. The reciprocal pledges sealed a circle that no intruder could break into. That night lit with burning stars. Our hearts pounded all night long.

Looking back, it was intuitive foresight that I had asked him to come. His friend converted to his side in the morning. He did not wait for me to leave before telling his mind. I was surprised at him because I expected him to say something light-hearted to ridicule our relationship. None of us told him about my imminent marriage to another man in less than a week's time. Rather, as we sat to take an early breakfast, which he insisted on before I left, he told us that our type of love could hurt as much as it thrilled us because of the anxiety we both suffered.

At home my uncle kept mum as if I had not disobeyed him, and did not ask where I had been before he left for work. He might only have been trying not to be late so as to arrive at work by the usual 9 a.m. Other nonjudicial government offices in the country opened for work at 8 a.m. Rachel also said nothing but only gazed at me now and then and twitched her right eye mischievously. She could imagine what I had experienced and did not ask me any questions.

I had promised Jo I would see him the following day, after my uncle left for work, and I did. We knew the relationship would be different after we parted this time. I would be Mrs. Anna Goomsay, no longer Miss Anna Dosang. Jo advised me to take the marriage seriously and he would like to hear about my success in life, which should gladden him.

"We must remain friends, even though I believe of a different kind from now on," he told me.

"Yes, we must," I said in tears as I embraced him.

"Do your best to make it work. I trust you will."

"Of course, I will always do my best."

He followed me to the road where I took a taxi. My heart weighed heavily in my chest while I waved and waved as he also waved and waved, his head bowed as if suppressing tears. I was beginning a new stage in life. I was going to be somebody's wife now in deed.

At home, Uncle Solomon still did not interrogate or punish me despite the flagrant insubordination. Whether he was biding his time or not, I could not tell. He uttered no reprimand and gave me, or rather Dr. Nathan Goomsay, his total support during the wedding, which took place five days later.

2

FAMILY TIES

My relationship with the young man who became both Dr. Nathan Goomsay and my husband had started indirectly before we met face to face. It all began as I was completing my studies in the secondary school. Ours was said to be the best girls' secondary school in the whole of BenuePlateau State then and that reputation rubbed off on all of its students. It was a unique school and we all felt fortunate to be students there. Though a very small town, Fiala had been chosen by the white missionaries as the headquarters of the Roman Catholic Mission, just as Zot was for the Sudan Interior Mission, which included the Anglican Church. There were three elementary schools there—one government-owned, the other two Catholic- and SIM-owned respectively. That was why our secondary school was established at Fiala, to be the seat of Western education in my area.

All the buildings in the school were painted pink on the outside and white inside. Pink and white were our school colors. Catholic reverend sisters had run the school since its opening in 1967. All of us at Our Lady of the Assumption Girls' Grammar School, Fiala, were excited at being cynosures of every male eye. Teenagers usually have a high opinion of themselves, and we were no exceptions to the rule. We were boisterous; our blood yearned for adventures. There was something in that later teen age that intoxicated like wine, and we were drunk with it. We wanted to be seen and admired in a rather innocent way. After all, none of us there knew the consequences of love; we did not know the aftermath of wedlock either.

I was the Queen of the Plateau whom every boy in the neighboring secondary school wanted to dance and chat with. I could see that in any social gathering I attended. I liked intelligent people, as I still do now.

Looks were not enough for me even at that tender age. We gossiped about our boyfriends and looked forward to any outing day when we would wear our white uniform and go out and introduce ourselves as students of OLAGGS. All of us were restless and the reverend sisters definitely knew. After all, though betrothed to the Catholic Church, they were human beings and, of course, women too. Many of them were relatively young, perhaps only in their late twenties or early thirties. Only two of them appeared old, the Principal called Sister Flannagan and the Vice-Principal, Sister O'Leary; both must have been in their mid-fifties.

Our dormitories were locked at 10 p.m. so that no student could sneak out to meet boys, as if they waited outside the gate all night. Mind you, not just the gate to the school compound, but the doors to each dormitory were locked till six in the morning. There were a few near cases of fire outbreaks that would have incinerated us all, but the school authorities still chose to have us locked in at night to preserve our chastity from preying hyenas! After all, we lived in savannah country. It was several years after I left Our Lady of the Assumption that fire broke out and killed twenty students before the practice of locking the doors was abandoned. We knew it was a stupid practice because the reverend sisters did not follow us home during vacation times. Should young girls be policed or taught to be responsible? At some stage in life one had to be responsible to oneself and to nobody else.

Nathan came from the nearby town of Kwaton; I from Nang—he from the hills and I from the plains. Times have passed when people really lived on the hilltops. The entire people had fled there during the war of horses and clashing swords against the turbaned chargers. The hills then provided refuge and protection from their enemies. Once the British had 'pacified' the different groups, the jihadists themselves stopped menacing the so-called heathen groups, who seized the opportunity of the cessation of hostilities to come down. And so, gradually, communities moved to the plains, which were really upland areas that were adequately drained ground. The plains were fertile lands. Later on in colonial times, the remaining hilltop settlements were deliberately burnt down to force the people down the plains to pay taxes to the British. The "hill people" settled at the foothills, quite a walk from the "people of the plains." The two towns needed each other and people from each attended the other's market.

Nathan's people were mainly hunters until recently; my people have always been farmers. We made fun of them as primitive—the women carried babies on their shoulders, not on their backs as we did. We saw them as dressing half-naked in sackcloth, unlike us who dressed in cotton clothes woven by our women.

The two towns fought wars a long time ago, according to the old, as to who should dominate the clan of five small towns and twenty-one villages. Farming land was relatively abundant, still each town or village wanted more for its people. People cherished merely pointing at a vast expanse of land, saying with relish: "It belongs to us." My father was fond of doing that. He was not ready to relinquish an inch of the land to another town; his own grandfather had fought to expand Nang's land. In the usually rocky landscape of the plateau, any green stretch of land was appreciated. Every stream was a blessing from the ancestors who would sneer at their offspring if they were not strong enough to defend their heritage. Land was not meant for farm alone, but also for grazing goats and sheep and for hunting. Who would give up the pack of animals in the bush to another town to hunt for its sustenance? Who would cede ample grazing fields to another town? The streams were rich in fishes that my people loved to eat.

Hundreds of people died because of the greed for more land to control. Intermittent skirmishes continued until the British came. The colonial officers studied their Intelligence Reports thoroughly and made neither town the district headquarters of Pandom but Fiala, which was smaller than each of them. Though there was still mistrust when I was

23

young, it was only recently that parents from one town would allow their children to marry from the other town. Nathan and I would not be the first from the two formerly hostile towns to marry, but such marriages were a recent development.

I did not hear about Nathan at school until my final year—he had left secondary school the previous year. When our two schools met earlier for debates, I participated but did not take notice of him. From what I would know about him, he preferred to go to the school laboratory than to spend his time listening to debates. We defeated his school and that caused a scandal in the district—the girls' school that defeated boys' schools in debates! I would learn with time that some types of men like Nathan and my respected uncle did not like to debate with women; they only wanted to dictate to them.

It was after he graduated from secondary school and got a state scholarship to go to Edinburgh to study Medicine that I heard his name mentioned frequently. I least expected that we would someday live together.

Before he left, as was common then, his parents wanted him to "point to a maid of his choice" whom he would like to marry later. His parents and relatives would approach the girl's parents and propose marriage of the two when their son returned. It did not occur to them that their son could marry before going overseas and take his wife along. Or, on the alternative, if they felt he was too young, he could complete his studies abroad, return, and then choose whom to marry. They did not even give him the opportunity to do the pointing, as custom demanded, but did it for him. What an abuse of the custom!

When I look back to those days, I laugh at the ludicrous arrangement. Raised in the culture like we were to respect our parents and our customs, we accepted what they asked us to do. And in daily life, there were many things we young ones did not like but had to do first and grumbled about afterwards. You could not challenge your parents because you respected them and because they knew, from experience, what you did not know. There was even a saying that what the elders forecast in the morning would come to pass later in the day. That made us to respect their foresight and wisdom.

Nathan's parents and relatives must have heard about me, a young lady about to leave secondary school, and a great debater who outshone boys in competitions. Our parents must have met in one ceremony or another and from a joke about becoming in-laws started the whole process behind our backs. The relationship between the inhabitants of the hills and those of the plains had warmed up in recent years. They attended each other's ceremonies, which were very many. Births brought naming ceremonies, deaths resulted in drinking and dancing orgies called funerals. Those who wanted to boost their egos acquired chieftaincy titles, and that called for parties. So, there were many opportunities for our parents to meet, socialize, and plan for the future of their children.

My father assumed that I would say "Yes," and did not care about my feelings and response. He reasoned that marrying was a girl's primary expectation and so saw the son of a potential chief and one going abroad for medical studies as an enviable match. My mother, who knew that somehow women among our people were always short-changed in marriage, asked me to obey and be wary.

"Get engaged traditionally and wait for him. Men change their feelings unpredictably. Then it will not be your fault to break what the two families have agreed upon and do what pleases you," she said.

"But how do I wait for somebody when I don't even know how long the waiting will be?" I asked.

She did not respond to my question directly, but said it was the women's lot to wait for men. I did not accept her reasoning, but felt that man and woman had to do their separate waiting for each other. I could not accept otherwise.

I had pen pals in America and Britain. I wrote them and they wrote back. They wrote about winter and snow, their strange seasons in which things appeared to be upside down. I wrote about the cool weather of our plateau, the rocks, trees, and the vast garden that stretched from one horizon to another. I envied their summers, as I believed they envied my all-year fantastic weather and beautiful landscape. I took it that this assumed proposal was also going to be a "write-write" relationship, a lot of correspondence that I was prepared for. I have always enjoyed writing letters to people I like, and find it the best way to maintain a relationship from a distance.

Somehow, I did not feel any fire as I had with my secret boyfriend whom I had to abandon. Francis attended Government College, Nassa, and was to drop out of school after his father died suddenly. He left the area to live with a distant cousin in Sokoto or Kano, and I never heard of or from him again. How could somebody be so close to a goal and abandon it? For a final-year student to drop out was painful. I was helpless, as I was not responsible for myself and there was no way of helping him. We had come close to playing intimately, but never ventured to exercise the burning appetite that we felt. I took it to be the work of fate. Fate—that kind and evil god!

My mother knew the Goomsays and had called me to her room for counseling.

"You know the importance of what's about to take place. When a girl grows up, she takes a man. Rather, a worthy man chooses her to be his wife. A girl must have honour lest the family will be shamed. It's time now for you to leave any other boy in your life."

I did not want to shame my family. But she did not understand my feelings. As arrangements for the ceremony of proposal drew near, I got scared.

"Can't this *burukutu* drinking ceremony wait until he comes back or when he visits?" I asked my mother.

26

"Life doesn't wait for anybody, especially not for us women. The son of one contesting to be chief and going to England will be a worthy husband. Take him, wait for him."

To her Edinburgh was in England, not Scotland. Wherever he was going, England or Scotland, was very far away. I did not like my mother's view of women. She who had advised me to be wary at the beginning had become a strong advocate of the son of the potential chief. It was most likely that Nathan's relatives had secretly brought her gifts, as was customary, and she had embraced their cause. She must be looking forward also to the gift of a goat from her son-in-law before the actual marriage would take place. Traditional suitors believed that once a young lady's mother was won over, the rest was a matter of time. They must have so lavishly treated my mother behind me that she became their best advocate for the engagement and eventual marriage. My mother then assumed that I had agreed to the proposal, brought indirectly to me via parents. It was the way they were used to, and it was the way they wanted to continue. She must have informed her senior brother, Uncle Solomon, who lived in Bukuru, about the proposal and he embraced it warmly. As my maternal uncle, his blessing in such things was traditionally sought.

I knew my father, who treated my mother like a glorified servant, would beat blood and tears out of her, if I refused to show up on the day of the engagement ceremony. Whenever I did anything remotely stubborn, rebellious, or wrong, my father blamed my action on my mother. He took it as if I was my mother and so should always obey every order from him. However, on a few occasions when I made him proud, he talked of "my good daughter" and forgot I was my mother's daughter too. At seventeen I had no mind and heart of my own, in his view of children, especially girls. I resented his assumptions that I must accept what pleased him, even if that hurt me.

My father did not have the personality of a man who could successfully manage a polygamous household. Or he had it in a very

27

canny way. He openly put down one woman before the other. He always nagged my mother for sending me to a secondary school, which made him to spend all the money he earned. His cultivation of millet and corn barely met our subsistence needs, but he talked about his farming as if he was earning so much. He reared no goats or sheep, which brought more money than crops. He refused to leave home and go to the tin mines to do what he called slave labor for money. He did not take kindly to the white people and their Hausa and Kanuri supervisors, all of whom were foreigners to him. So, his spending all his money on me was not true, since my uncle, the magistrate, virtually paid my school fees. My father gave me very little towards my upkeep. But with that type of statement, he made my mother's rival jealous. And my mother was proud to be the mother of the only child in the entire street, and a girl at that, who was going to college.

That evening of the engagement ceremony, Nathan did not even come with his relatives. My father was host and his large sitting room and the open air in the rectangular compound would seat the main guests and other uninvited people. Like every other ceremony around, we had to provide for more than the invited guests. Really, not invited guests but the elders of the two families who were expected to be the main participants of the ceremony.

Children had raided nearby compounds and brought in cushion and other types of chairs. Women had painted the walls of the compound, with brown mud and they shone. I wish our compound had always been as glossy. Our compound, like others around, was rectangular in shape. At the center was a large courtyard around which stood homes and huts of various sizes. The round huts were meant for the ancestral shrine, food store, kitchen, goats, and other uses. The homes were rectangular and roofed with zinc. I believe my maternal uncle contributed to the zinc roofing, which replaced the thatched one. My father had his house near to the entrance, and from this strategic position he was able to protect the entire family. Our houses faced the west or south, but not the east from where winds bring heavy and violent rainfall or the north from where winds blow dust and cold between November and February. Cactuses demarcated our compound from others.

Nathan's family brought tins of the local brew and baskets of kola nuts. His family spokesperson explained that their son had traveled to Kaduna for his visa to England and had not returned. His presence was not important, they surmised—they were about to extract a pledge or oath from me without the person for whom it was being done! I was called to the assembly when members of the two families were already bloodshot in their eyes. The women had been quartered separately. They were twice as many as the men who had thrice their share of *burukutu* beer and kola nuts! And they sat in a circle on mats in the open compound; only men sat in the sitting room.

One of the elderly-looking women in the group called me to their circle. She was big-boned, in her fifties, and with big eyes. Jema was used to this ceremony and presided over it with delight. She dropped out of elementary school but was respected in the village for having gone to school at all. She had a smattering of broken English with which she impressed her illiterate mates. She was leader of the married women and both young and old deferred to her. She called out to me and I stepped into the circle and sat down like they were to show my respect. "This is not a marriage yet," she lectured me.

"Behave well through school and university and our son will marry you. From now on, you are his fiancee," she told me.

The women clapped hands and took up a song in praise of marriage and the children that would come from it.

It is with children that life is enjoyed
It is with children that life is enjoyed
Children cover you more than any blankets

29

Children are the greatest wealth It is
with children that life is enjoyed It is
with children that life is enjoyed.

To them, marriage was a practical union meant to make children.
And woe betides the married woman who does not conceive within two
years or so of marriage! But this was not a marriage yet to prove my
fertility. I would wait, chaste, for my would-be-husband to be ready to
have me. The man was not expected to be chaste or wait for only me. It
was an unfair pact that our women had been forced to accept from the
beginning. The men could not see this unfairness.

Some elder, hand shaking from a combination of age and drinks,
prayed over a cup of the drink and kola nut, which he passed to me.
Taking the drink and the kola nut obligated me to be Nathan's wife-to-be.
I never liked *burukutu*, the millet beer, which made my people leave their
work early for drinking sprees at the male joints. The local brew definitely
made them behave in a frenetic and irresponsible way. I took the cup and
passed it to my mother. Nobody challenged me for not drinking, since
many of us young ladies did not drink it. I bit, chewed, and swallowed the
lobe of kola nut. I was not conscious of taking an oath that was too
onesided. The usual ululation followed from the women who sang away
our freedom without knowing.

Who is the newest bride-to-be?
Who is the newest bride-to-be?
It is Anna, it is Anna; it is Anna.
The college one who can speak English!
She is the true beauty that distracts men,
They knock a tree stump out of their way.
Who is the newest bride-to-be?
Who is the newest bride-to-be?

30

It is Anna, it is Anna; it is Anna.
The college one who can speak English!

By the time Nathan returned from Kaduna, he had barely thirty minutes to visit me. I lived with my mother in her room and she stepped out when he came in. We knew she wanted to give us a chance to be free with ourselves. Nathan was pressed hard for time. He had to go home to prepare for his flight the following day from Kano. He would sleep in Bukuru and take a taxi from there to Kano for the one o'clock LagosKano-London Heathrow Nigerian Airways flight. He was dressed in a funny way. It might be in anticipation of going to Britain; he wanted to get used to wearing a suit. Or was it that he did not change his interview dress before he came to see me? He had a locally sewn brown suit that he looked awkward in. He did not wear a tie, which would have made him look crazy to me.

He looked at me and felt I must be excited that he was going abroad. He was rather serene. How mature, he looked at twenty. The onset of his balding had started—at least the signs were visible on his large forehead. At five six, he was average in height, plump as a well-fed young man. He must be very intelligent to get a scholarship, not many students who applied got it. I waited for his move. What was he going to tell me? We sat opposite each other. His eyes bulged a little and suited his face well. If I were the one going to Britain the next day for the first time in my life, everybody would hear my heart beat a loud drum.

He showed no endearments, no excitement about me as a woman, no outpourings of love. I did not blame him for what I perceived as his lukewarm attitude because we had barely known each other. We gazed as if each was gauging the other emotionally. We were not yet in love. It was something we had to start cultivating. I volunteered a question to break the silence.

"When do you leave?"

31

"In fact, in a few minutes. My father said I must see you before leaving," he told me.

I was infuriated that he came because his father asked him to see me. If his father did not insist, he would not have come to see me. But I couldn't blame him. He might be as lukewarm as I was toward the whole arrangement. But he should have created more time for us to get used to one another. I felt like a prisoner of war; I hoped I would not continue to be held against my will. A potential student of medicine had won the Queen of the Plateau! I was confused within. Would love grow with time or was it already stillborn? I prayed that love should grow to swathe both of us in one home. When I got used to him, I promised myself, I would do my best to make the love to bloom. But I had no illusions that its growth had to be from reciprocal nursing by both man and woman.

I promised to write him as often as he would write me. He would send me pictures of snow and himself in winter dress, he said. He would write about Trafalgar Square, Kensington Palace, and Hyde Park that he had read about. At the British Consulate in Kaduna, he told me, he had spent his long waiting time before the short interview reading the London brochure. Then, who knew the difference between London and Edinburgh? After all, the Queen's husband was the Duke of Edinburgh.

And so we parted without touching each other—neither a handshake nor an embrace. I was apprehensive of Nathan, as he might have been of me too. I felt I was being stampeded into a fenced lot. I feared how I would fare in the enclosure.

Many girls in my school, especially those from my hometown, heard about my traditional engagement to a student of medicine in Britain, and envied my position. I must have been the subject of gossip in the dormitories. Some of my fellow senior students told me before the West African School Certificate examination that I did not need to pass. My future was already secure, they told me.

"What else do you need in life if a doctor's wife?" asked Jummai, who always took pleasure in talking about relationships and questioning her classmates and friends about their boyfriends and suitors.

She had no boyfriend of her own and, from her carefree behavior and poor dressing, did not make any effort to attract men. "You are already in heaven on earth," she stated.

"Why do you think that I should not become a doctor, journalist, or some professional myself?" I asked.

"I no de that one-o," she replied.

"Why do I need to work, if my husband can bring in so much money?" she asked back.

"What if things don't go right?" I asked.

"I must please am-o," she said, and others burst out laughing.

It was the harmattan period, towards the end of the school year in early December, and we talked, laughed, and busied ourselves to keep warm. Since it was cold and windy outside, we tended to remain indoors and that was an opportunity for "girl-talk," sheer gossip. How they got to know Nathan Goomsay's name only God knows. Or they had good spies. "Hello, Mrs. Goomsay!" Jummai would greet me.

"When are we having the bridal shower?" her talkative roommate Margaret asked.

I usually did not reply, but I felt this was a chance to put things right.

"I am only engaged, not yet about to marry," I told both of them as I walked away.

The inquisitive senior students pried into my mails as if only Nathan wrote me. They imagined whenever my British or American pen pal wrote to be Nathan's letter. I was so exasperated once with them that I had to throw Mike Smith's letter at them so that they could read about snow and avalanches!

"It's not only Nathan who lives in Britain, and I have pen friends there," I shouted at them.

Debra and Josephine had always been true friends. They did not take part in romanticizing my engagement. They cautioned our schoolmates behind me about the unnecessary harassment, which gradually fizzled out.

I started to expect Nathan's letter or postcard a week after he left. I was restless and confused about the engagement and wanted his words in letters to calm the turbulence in me. Those were days when telegrams and letters traveled fast and safe. Neither telegram nor letter came from my fiance. That was just before the end-of-school examinations. If I knew his address, I would have written him—it would have relieved me a bit. But he promised to write me as soon as he arrived there. I wrote my exams with a hard-beating heart, anxious to hear from my family-sanctioned fiancé. I received letters from my British pen pal in the same London or Edinburgh where he was supposed to now live. When an aerogramme letter arrived, I always guessed that Nathan had at long last broken his silence, but for six months I was always wrong.

I went to stay at home in Nang after the final examinations. I could have stayed in Bukuru with my uncle, but I wanted to wait for Nathan's letter at home. I had been admitted for a four-year degree programme in English/Mass Communication at the University of Yerwa. I had started to curse my fate for presenting myself at the traditional engagement. My thoughts ran wild into hundreds of possibilities. This would be the shortest-lived engagement I had known. Did he foresee this problem; hence he was not with his family at the ceremony, which emphasized more of alcohol consumption than anything else? Had he lost memory of his native Pandom and me? People could change fast, and he might have turned his back on what he left at home. His parents wondered about this also and came to me to ask if their son had written me. I would, for a long time, be tied to his family rather than to the person that I was preparing to marry someday.

He wrote six months later, not directly to me but to his father whom he asked to give his address to me and to his friends in town. I was not very sure whether I was mentioned in the letter and wondered whether it was not his father who wanted to be courteous to me. This shocked me, since he knew my address—any letter to anybody in Nang got delivered through one postal agency box or another. I put my shock and anger behind me and still wrote him asking how he was faring, his health, studies, and everything abroad. I also wrote about my preparations to go to the University of Yerwa and what I intended to study there. I received Nathan's first letter after I wrote him, and that was eight months after our engagement and his parting to Britain.

The letter itself was brief. Again, he did not ask about how I was faring, nor what I would do after our examinations. There was no display of emotions about missing me, nor any expression of affection. He said nothing about his own studies. It was late spring or early summer there and he sent pictures in which he was feeding pigeons in Trafalgar Square amidst a crowd of tourists. He must have been visiting London from Edinburgh. He ended with "Yours sincerely, Nathan." I expected much more than "Yours sincerely" from him and would always expect far more than the very little he gave me in feelings and other things that I needed in order to be fulfilled.

3

THREE FRIENDS

Of the three of us friends, I was the first to be betrothed traditionally. I mocked myself when we were together. I was the goat tethered to a tree for sacrifice to a god that enjoyed the sight of blood.

Debra did not go through the engagement ritual that I had undergone. Good that she did not, but went straight into a relationship with Edmund Pudap. They had gone far— living together for almost a year—before they told their parents who quickly arranged a traditional marriage ceremony before my friend would be pregnant, or, if already with child, before the sex exhibit would show boldly.

In Bukuru and neighboring towns and villages, Christians and Muslims watched each other closely, spied on the other's lifestyle, and used one side's weakness to promote its group's strength. If a Christian girl got pregnant before marriage, it was to the Muslims' pleasure—a strong point against the wayward nature of Christianity, a religion they derided as condoning prostitution. Similarly, if a Muslim girl conceived outside of marriage, the Christians gloated over the mishap or misstep as showing the hypocrisy of her religious group. Each side wanted to take advantage of the other to advance its faith. The Christians sent their girls to school in accordance with the then new universal free primary education law. Some Muslim parents did not, though most broke ranks with the faithful and did. One of the arguments of Muslim parents was that Western education corrupted women, and unmarried pregnant Christian girls would prove their point. But among the young women of our time, Muslim or Christian, we hid to seek pleasure if at all we wanted to, and if one conceived it was a matter of bad luck.

Josephine and I attended the marriage ceremony and we were oddly happy for our friend, oddly so because we knew that all three of us were so scared of marriage. Had we not seen our mothers, always toiling for their children and husbands, going to bed last and getting up first, preparing and serving food while young ones and "old babies" of husbands waited greedily to fill their hunger? Were we not taught to sing about the woman who died of hunger and happily so, after giving all to sustain her husband and children? For men, the hero was one who had shot or killed a wild animal such as a leopard or a lion. For women, the heroine was the one who died in the process of caring for her child or husband. The roles were not just or fair—only women made sacrifices for the benefit of their men. When would men make sacrifices for the pleasure of their women? Did we not see the young married women age so rapidly within a few years as to lose their youth and luster? Who would recognize those slender waists only three years into marriage and already two babies? There appeared to be a conspiracy of nature and men to rob women of their beauty.

"If it comes my way, I don't know whether I will have the patience or stamina to be wife," Josephine confided.

"Marriage, like everything else in life, has to be tried," Debra said.

"I am afraid of what I have, though others could be luckier with theirs," I told my friends.

"You are either in or out of it," Debra stated categorically.

Of the three of us, she was the most forceful then. She appeared determined in whatever she wanted to do, unlike Josephine and I who dealt with every issue like chameleons treading cautiously before peril ahead. In fact, Debra had warned us that caution would not necessarily save us from mishap, if that happened to be our destiny.

Josephine and I knew that Debra was going to throw herself into the marriage with all her body, mind, and soul. She preferred very bright colors—her clothes, shoes, and handbags were red, blue, black, or white. She liked them solid, and we knew what to give her as gifts—the very colors that she loved, two sets of wrappers, one green and the other blue with the handbags and shoes to match them. She loved them.

Debra did not practice moderation. She either refused to drink or took what we considered too much for a woman. She drank wine, whiskey, and brandy in large draughts.

"That's why you'll remain men's slaves," she would say, as if possessed. "What's too much for a woman that's not too much for a man? Why do you condemn yourself over what you would absolve others from?"

Her questions enlightened, but worried us. She was the one in marriage, the first of us friends to marry, at least live with a man, and yet the one not accepting the role already plotted for her as wife.

In the midst of the drinking and dancing, the elders of the two families called our friend and her belated husband-to-be for the crucial ceremony. Being the dry season and hot inside, the ceremony was held in the open air. The elders formed a semi-circle and Debra stood facing the seated representatives of the two families. Dong, the spokesperson of her family, stood up and raised his embroidered fan to draw everybody's attention. He was so tall and rather slim that he was often compared to a slender *neem* tree. Dong beckoned on Debra to come closer and asked her to face her soon-to-be husband. What a ridiculous thing, this husband-to-be when they had been living together for so long!

"We have received the cow and five goats that your prospective husband has sent to us. He also sent a sixth goat to your mother and another cow to your mother's relations and they are here to show their appreciation. He has done what our people expect of an honorable man," he said before the assembly of the two families.

He paused for a moment, as he looked around the many people present at the ceremony. It was a gesture to show that he was very impressed by the high attendance of the marriage. Fried meat, beni-seed cake, and *burukutu*, the local beer, were in abundance. Dong again settled his gaze on Debra.

"Do what your man tells you," he instructed.

He paused for a long moment, as if to allow Debra to contradict him if she wanted to. But she knew that no woman was expected to counter that instruction before the elders lest their displeasure would ensure an evil spell that could haunt her all her life.

"Give him as many children as he wants, make him happy, take good care of him at the expense of your own comfort," he further told her.

Then facing his fellow elders of both families, Dong called on Mr. Pudap to stand beside Debra. They had worn the same type of blue brocade. It was the trend for the bride and bridegroom to dress that way.

"Have I spoken the right words of our fathers?" Dong asked. "Yeaaah," the men yelled and reinforced the affirmation by nodding their heads.

"Take your wife and go away with her," he instructed Mr. Pudap.

As instructed and as custom demanded, Edmund Pudap held Debra by the hand and made to take her away while Dong then stepped back to his seat among the elders. A mock battle of several young men attempting to seize Debra took place. As custom also demanded, Mr. Pudap threatened them physically and they fled, leaving the bride with her rightful groom. The contract had been made. We were surprised that our friend not only nodded in agreement to the unfair contract, but also said "Yes" aloud. To our disappointment, while Debra was asked to be faithful, the man was put under no such obligation of fidelity.

Later, the old women took their turn instructing our newlywed friend on what to do and not do as a married woman. They were very satisfied with the food and drinks around. They sat on mats at their end of the prepared ground.

"Except when under menstruation, don't deny your husband pleasure of your body."

"Always get his food ready on time when he wants it."

"Keep him neat all the time."

"Help him to be prosperous."

"His health is your health."

"Don't be jealous."

"Don't you ever strike him. It is forbidden for a woman to strike a man or bring him to the ground."

"Don't ever look at another man with desire."

"Report to him what any other man tells you."

"Don't keep the company of bad women."

"Help your husband to save, make no unnecessary demands."

By the time they had completed reciting the litany of responsibilities of the wife, it appeared her husband had nothing to do in marriage than be attended to as her lord. The men did not publicly recite to the groom a litany of responsibilities as done to the bride. The same customs that demanded brides to be publicly instructed, I understand, expected the man to be patient and calm. The man was also expected to control his anger and to provide for his wife. I wished these commandments were repeated before the two families as witnesses of an even contract! Women could be their own tormentors, I felt. They sowed the seeds of guilt in their young ones and absolved men from the same. I was only engaged and discovered here that the instructions I was given at the family gathering were mild compared to the real marriage commands.

Debra was serene at the marriage oath-taking ceremony. She had to come in to change from the blue attire to a white head-tie, a white brocade blouse, and a white *george* wrapper. She wore white shoes and had a white handbag to match. Fine as she looked, there was disdain for the whole exercise that only those of us who knew her well saw in her comportment.

As soon as the prolonged ceremony was over, she rejoined Josephine and me in her room. Her father had kept that room for her and nobody used it until she visited. She decorated it with pictures of stars, male and female, including Eddie Murphy, Bob Marley, Tina Turner, and Patti Boulet. In the fairly big room were two brown-upholstered chairs and a big iron bed. Debra threw off all the clothes she had worn on the floor and put on a regular *boubou* dress. She sat on the bed and faced us sitting on the chairs. "I hope I was not like a masquerade?" she asked. We did not answer her. Instead, we stared at her, as if she were a stranger.

"Why do both of you look so mystified because of this?" she asked.

Again, we were silent. Debra dismissed the traditional exercise as a "party declaration" that could not hold her from doing what pleased her. She said she would be Mrs. Debra Pudap for as long as her husband remained tied to her waist, as she would be to his. If he got loose and wandered from her, she would show him that she had more power and options than he had. She laughed off our fears, brought out bottles of Guinness she had kept for our three-some party. She turned on her boom box to play reggae music, which we all loved so much. We danced and joked about ourselves. Who was going to be commander-in-chief of her household? Who would be the sacrificial goat? Who would be the mythical mother who died to save her children and husband from hunger? We asked questions without answering them. The Guinness no doubt made us lighter than normal. We tried to talk around the real question that we needed to ask ourselves, "Why should women be second-class citizens in their societies?" Had things been always so? Or somewhere in history, before the coming of Europeans, our women were equal to men? What should women do to be equal with men? Later in the university I would read Buchi Emecheta's poignant novels about the injustices done to women.

That was many years ago. I married in spite of my fears. I feared the man I wanted to marry. I feared marriage itself. But for some reasons, I wanted to taste the experience. Would it be sweet or bitter, or something in-between? What would I do to make it really sweet? Nathan did not give me any opportunity to savor sweetness. The draughts of bitterness started very early. Soon they became tasteless, and then I wanted to throw up. But I soon got entrapped in the child-making reality of marriage, which I did not realize early enough would complicate my matrimonial ties with Nathan.

I thought of my friends. Josephine left for Lagos, a bold move, to work far from home. It was very reasonable of her to run away from the

41

boa constrictors of men at home. Maybe outside would be more relaxed for living. She got a job at British Caledonia Airlines, which later merged with British Airways. She started by issuing tickets, then checking passengers for boarding. She traveled abroad for vacations and had seen much of the outside world that Debra and I had not seen, but only dreamed of. When she offered me a ticket, my husband would not let me take the offer.

"How do you follow a single woman to travel abroad? Do you understand what it means to be married?" he shouted.

"Is she not my friend? Did I not know her before I knew you?" I asked.

"That she is your friend does not change her status as a spinster," he told me.

He had no respect for me, none for my friends. I knew he would pour insults on my friend, if I continued arguing. He was not the sort of person who listened to two sides of an argument and accepted the more persuasive side. He barked out orders and always expected to be obeyed.

I had thought of a true vacation, unlike my following him to the village where I slaved to please everybody at my disconcerting expense. He asked me to take foodstuff along and I cooked to feed those we visited. What hospitality, Kwaton style! He said that this was the culture, but was it fair for me to be the guest and yet the one to treat my hosts? I soon resented following him home. Did he think that he could not live without my obeying antiquated customs? Or he feared I might not return if I traveled abroad? I did not think he was jealous at the beginning, but he wanted me to be always within his beck and call to exasperate, wear out, or humiliate to satisfy his lordship over me.

I had offers of foreign trips over three times and they were all turned down with harsh barking. I believe Josephine understood his feelings and has not for the past ten years suggested that I accompany her

42

to London, Rome, New York, or Amsterdam. I could only dream of flights to his village in a worn-out car!

Josephine has not married to this day. She had risen to be the Passengers Manager at the main office of British Airways in Victoria Island. She lived in the exclusive Beach Towers and drove a BMW car. I could not accept her invitations to visit her in Lagos either—my dog would bark out and kill whatever he felt would give me pleasure or make me free. I started to see marriage as a prison house of torture. Josephine insisted she would not marry, but would not mind having relationships. And many relationships she has had, breaking up when she found her partners irresponsible or no longer loving. She insisted that a relationship was a two-way traffic that needed reciprocal maintenance from both sides.

Josephine and I were not surprised at the breakup of our friend's marriage. Debra had only behaved according to nature. The marriage was either good or bad; it worked or failed. If good, she stayed in it and if bad she left. She was not a punch bag for a man to strike at and relieve his rage. She was not going to be a cow to follow the butcher to the slaughterhouse either. She did not wait to be pushed outside, her belongings thrown into the front yard, as was common in many places. As she told us later, she warned her man many times that she knew her rights and how to exercise them if she wanted. After the traditional marriage, they went to the Court Registry to fill and sign marriage forms; in fact, they married twice.

The man slept outside with impunity and sometimes went to work from where he slept.

"Either you are for me and with me or you are not," she told him.

"Since when did you become the commander-in-chief of my house?" he asked. "If it is your house, I'll leave it and get my own," Debra warned.

Mr. Pudap did not expect her to have the will to leave on her own. But he got the shock of his life. Debra made every arrangement necessary ahead of leaving.

"If you sleep outside again, you will not come to meet me in *your* house!"

And she kept to her threat. Mr. Pudap ignored her threat and slept outside again. She broke away and moved to an apartment in Diobu quarter of Port Harcourt. She soon dropped the Pudap part of her name for her father's name—Kuan. In the long letter describing the steps she had taken to free herself, as she put it, she flung Pudap back at the dog! She was proud of being Miss Kuan again. She was doing fine teaching at the State University. She had taken a Master's degree in Theatre Arts and was working on a Ph.D. degree as she taught. She promised to work hard to achieve a status that would be higher than Mr. Edmund Pudap's so as to avoid being laughed at. Divorced men were always watching how their former spouses fared, and for the most part many did not fare well and that gave them pleasure.

"I will be higher than him in this Port Harcourt," Debra had sworn.

She was driven hard to succeed by this challenge she threw before him. She wanted to be the one to laugh at him, rather than the other way around. Debra always confounded expectations, and I knew she would do all it took to rise to the highest position in the university some day to come.

So here was I, embattled between a torturer and a healer, between a husband and a lover. No doubt from the code of conduct meant for wives and the freedom of men, many women might be in the same position as mine. I knew Debra would frown at my stealing out to meet my friend Jo whom she knew and admired. She would advise me to walk out of the marital home, absolve myself from the oaths that our elders conducted and go out free to embrace whom I loved in the marketplace. Josephine would concur with her. But would my patience change the situation? With children already in the marriage, would it be fair for them if I left and we started a custody battle that would cause trauma for them? Was Nathan bad or the old customs in which he was raised had so affected him that he wanted things to be as they had always been in the village? I settled for patience for the time being and to make every effort possible to bring Nathan to me. Who knows? He might be looking for ways himself to bring me closer? I would not choose the easy way out of this. But will effort and patience boil a stone to be soft like yam? I waited for the result.

4

SETTLING DOWN

After our wedding, I had to move to Barkin Ladi, where Nathan lived. He had set up a clinic fifteen kilometers away in a small rural town, Rof, and drove there to work every day. I had asked him why he did not live where his clinic was and he had responded that the place was almost a village and he could not live in any village except his own Kwaton. My reasoning that it would be better to live beside his clinic fell on deaf ears. I also surmised he wanted to work hard during the day and relax after work. After all, many physicians burn themselves out from the stress of the profession. He would still be on call from Barkin Ladi if there were an emergency, but living in Rof by the clinic would be a busier matter. Who knows, he might want more time to spend with his family and staying away from the clinic to avoid unncessary intrusion made sense. Soon, though, I became used to Barkin Ladi and it fitted well into my own academic ambition.

I had for long nursed the idea of going for further studies. Just before I married, I resigned from teaching at Girls' Secondary School, Bukuru. It was not that Bukuru was too far away. If I wanted to continue teaching in the secondary school, it would not have been too much of a problem to commute daily to and from Bukuru. Nathan wanted me to work in the civil service, but I did not like the sedentary life involved in sitting in the office from eight to four. I was more of the restless kind that teaching suited more than any other job. So, I wanted to pursue higher studies with a view to still teach but perhaps at a higher level.

After my first child, Dauda, was born, I thought I could start further studies. However, without being planned for, I became pregnant again when Dauda was not yet eighteen months. I had Dauda and Patrick within two and a half years of marriage. I knew that once the children were a little grown up, I had to start preparation for graduate studies before it was too late for me to do so. And so, as soon as they were two and three and a half years old respectively, I made the necessary application to enter the graduate program. I was not sure I would be allowed to start the doctoral program immediately, so I put "MA/Ph.D" for my desired program. Then I did not know that there was the limbo of M.Phil. for those who could not go ahead to the Ph.D. stage after the M.A. After my admission into the graduate school, I had to go to The University of Bukuru to register for studies. This would be very tasking, as I had to combine the roles of wife, mother, and student in one. Fortunately, I was admitted into the research program, which did not need my attendance of lectures. With a good supervisor, Dr. Kunle Ayorinde, I was able to go through proposal presentation and writing stages without having to be on campus on a daily basis. I had to commute from Barkin Ladi to Bukuru only on the days I had to be in the university campus to submit an assignment.

Those were really hard days. I did not have a car then and Nathan was too busy with his to give it to me to drive even to the market. Nathan went to his clinic on weekdays and some days I went to Bukuru. The bus service from Barkin Ladi to Bukuru was very regular and cheap, but often congested. The buses were usually not in a good condition with the state of the national economy. Bus owners or their drivers put off servicing their vehicles for as long as possible and usually bought cheap or Taiwan brands of spare parts for the overdue maintenance. So, many times, the buses broke down and I had to take another one because no driver refunded

46

money once you had paid your fare. I was very busy, since on such days that I went to the University of Bukuru, I still had to walk the children to the kindergarten school and returned from the university before their school closed at five.

Nathan was very supportive of me when I told him about my interest in furthering my education.

"That should be fine," he said.

"Thanks for your support," I told him.

The support though was temporary. It was as if he grudgingly approved of my studies because he suspected that I was bent on having a Ph.D. anyway. He started to show displeasure after he found out that I was really serious. He had perhaps thought that I would be worn out by the rigor of commuting and studies and so would abandon the program. But there I was doggedly waking early, giving him food, then leaving for Bukuru, and returning before his dinner.

"What do you need an M.A. or Ph.D. for?" he asked one day. I had thought I was carrying him along to develop myself as he did himself with his medical profession. I tried to make him happy after he came from work so that he could be cheerful with me. The first few weeks after marriage, I always ran out to meet him as he came back from work and took from him his briefcase. He surrendered it a few times, but later would not. Once in the house, I gave him a glass of cold water. I felt he needed to cool down before taking food or doing anything else in the house. I then asked him about his work for the day. I received no formal training on how to be a wife and, because of our cool relationship in the long years of engagement, I wanted to make some effort to make things work. Did Jo not tell me to put in my best and be a good wife? I wanted to see what being a good wife was. Within a few weeks, my advances were rejected.

"What are you up to with coming to take my briefcase? Don't bother again," he told me.

I got the message. I wanted him to warm up to me and I to him. Not many men supported their wives to do graduate studies and I had to commend Nathan, however grudging his approval had been. Even when displeased with the idea of my having a Ph.D., he did not physically stop me from going to school. I did much of my research in the library and so had the primary texts I wanted. I got a few books on theories and concepts such as feminism, modernism and postmodernism, post-colonialism, social organizations, and patriarchy. As long as I did not travel to Yerwa, where he thought Jo was then, he was fine at the beginning. I received some books from Jo in Lagos, where he was already an associate professor. Time flies so fast that in four and a half years, I was able to defend my dissertation on "African Women Writers' Response to Patriarchy" without any problem. I studied Ama Ata Aidoo, Buchi Emecheta, Ifeoma Okoye, and Bessie Head. Nathan refused to follow me to the University the day I defended my dissertation, but I brought him the news of my successful defense, without any excitement on his part. I suddenly realized that he might not like my being called Dr. Goomsay, just like him. It was an equality that he would resist. So, there was no party for me for bagging a Ph.D. in English.

Fortunately, Barkin Ladi had the State Polytechnic and my supervisor knew both the Head of General Studies and the Rector of the institution. He must have noticed that I was forgetful and not cheerful most of the time and, to my surprise, had suggested that I took up a job to keep me more occupied from non-domestic chores. He must have put in a good word for me to the authorities in the State Polytechnic because my degrees were in literature and not language that was more marketable in such an institution. The interview had been fixed suddenly for the following day and I had not been to school for days. Professor Ayorinde frantically looked for me but did not know where I lived. He had heard about my husband's clinic and he drove there. When he asked to see Dr. Goomsay, he was taken to him. The physician looked at him with suspicion. This couldn't be Jo, he must have thought in his mind. Professor Ayorinde introduced himself as Anna Goomsay's dissertation supervisor. But that did not make Dr. Goomsay to tell him to sit down. The professor had expected that his student's husband would be excited to see him. But he was left standing and not even asked why he came. He thought it was the pressure of work and decided to leave. Behold, just at the entrance to the clinic he met me as I arrived there to get medication for Dauda who was coughing persistently. He told me about the interview and I hurriedly went in to tell my husband, then rushed out to meet the professor and we drove off.

The Rector was very pleased to employ me. I was employed even before I completed the application and asked three references to be sent in on my behalf. Professor Ayorinde did me a great favor. The teaching position was very convenient for me because, although I had to take a taxi to work daily, it was not expensive because of the fairly short distance. There was no traditional English Department, but communication, literature, language, and technical writing were taught together as English in the General Studies Department. The department was more of a service one, but that did not deter my enthusiasm to teach in it. I would try to integrate more literature into the curriculum that existed, I told myself. I was elated and I wanted to work hard from Lecturer II to one day becoming a Chief Lecturer.

The night of the day that I did the interview and got employed, Nathan questioned me about "that man." He told me that he must be my lover and had come to ask of me even from him! I explained to him that he was my supervisor and had come to tell me to attend an interview that was hastily arranged for me at the State Polytechnic. He laughed mischievously and asked me whether I thought he was a fool.

"And you jumped into his car and drove away to God-knowswhere!"

I told him that he had to trust me, but he again laughed cynically. For days he would not talk to me because of Professor Ayorinde and mumbled sarcastic things to himself. He was jealous of any man that had contact with me.

I started work within two weeks of the successful interview. To my dismay, the female lecturers at The State Polytechnic, Barkin Ladi, were very few, indeed only seven of us out of more than eighty lecturers. And four of us were from the State. Why this gender imbalance? What inhibited our women from going to school? Or, if they did go, why did they not aspire to higher degrees and teach in polytechnics and universities? Of the four of us from the State, I was the only one with a Ph.D. degree; another had Ed.D. in Physics and the other two had M.Ed. in Mathematics and Chemistry respectively.

From the beginning, I nursed the idea of making a change. Many of my male counterparts in the General Studies Department felt uneasy with me for no just reason. It was not only those without Ph.Ds but even those who had the same qualification and had far more experience in teaching than me a beginner in the profession. However, I just wanted to do my work well and make an impact on the students we had. Was the resistance to women everywhere? The patriarchy I had studied was rearing its ugly head in the department as in my home.

The students were majoring in science and technology subjects, but they still needed General Studies to round up their degrees. Everybody needs to communicate effectively, scientist or technologist. I would do my best to teach them express themselves succinctly and also make the few literature books I taught touch their hearts and souls. The scientist with a tender heart could contribute immensely to humanity, I assumed. If the likes of my man had studied more literature, especially that of a sensitive nature, he might have become a far more likeable person, I thought. It was my duty to teach and help towards a humanity that enriched science.

It took me six months in The State Polytechnic to start a Women's Creative Writing Club. I wanted to tread slowly though, lest I be accused of being too active; hence I wanted only female students, lecturers, and administrative staff to be members. Women needed to be mobilized to function collectively. Having men in the club would have made it too large and I really wanted us women to freely express our condition as women without inhibition. The presence of men would have defeated that objective.

The inaugural meeting was well attended. Twenty-five women were in attendance. I knew from experience of clubs and societies from my student days at Yerwa that some would inevitably drop out, but whatever number remained would still be sizable enough for a writing club. We introduced ourselves and talked about our separate interests. Many already wrote poetry, and others were interested in short stories and plays. I was highly elated and would make sure that we gave each other the necessary support to blossom in our separate writings.   I was elected president and patron of the Club. We met the first Tuesday of the month at 5 p.m. in the Female Hostel A's lounge. Many poems and short stories would come to life because of this support group. Later it was affiliated with the Association of Nigerian Authors, Plateau Branch.

Out of the blue, I received an invitation from the National Organization of Women (NOW) in Abuja to attend their annual meeting. That was a year after I started teaching at The State Polytechnic. I could not make it, but wrote of my interest in joining the association and attending future meetings if I had the chance. Shortly thereafter, we had a NOW branch at the Polytechnic campus. Our aim was to raise the overall awareness of students and especially young women so that they could become self-reliant adults. There was a lot of confidence in the air that our women would one day be as great achievers as men already were. We visited secondary schools and talked to the girls, encouraged them to form drama groups and act out their experiences.

I lived daily with problems at home. I wrestled constantly with the confusion that had wracked my heart since I met Jo and which had intensified since my marriage. How could I now act as a good mentor and a role model, divided as I was in my heart? Jo was not around but I felt his presence daily. Nathan was there with me but would not take me into his bosom. I kept my feelings inside and they did not seem to show in my teaching or participation in both the writers' club and NOW.

Professor Ayorinde and his wife came to visit me months after I started work. He had introduced his wife to me and he expected both of us to be friends. He encouraged me to write, as he saw productivity as the key to success in an academic career. Though it was a Saturday, Nathan had been out and came in as he was driving off. When I told him who had visited, he said that he did not want any professor or his wife in our house again. He said I was using the professor's wife for a cover. Cover for what, he did not explain.

I wrote papers with the encouragement of both Jo and Professor Ayorinde. The old professor literally treated me as a daughter and spurred me on with my writing. I certainly didn't think I was doing anything extraordinary than just performing my duties at The State Polytechnic. However, it appeared I was being noticed everywhere on the campus and in all of Barkin Ladi. My so-called hard work drew the attention of the Head of General Studies Department and the Rector. I was promoted fairly fast to Lecturer I in two years of teaching. It appeared that I was on a fast track in my academic career. I felt inspired to work even harder.

Nathan learned of my performance in my workplace and it seemed he was not happy with it. He felt the State Polytechnic's Rector was interested in me romantically, hence he was doing everything possible to promote me. For some days, he no longer talked about Professor Ayorinde, whom he knew was in another institution and relatively far away. I was becoming too visible or being heard of too much and that seemed to enrage him. The women's affairs editor of *The Standard*,

Margaret Duru, came to the campus to interview me and later wrote a fine piece on women in higher institutions of learning with my picture there. I was getting popular and a housewife was not supposed to be so.

I appeared on television in a discussion panel on The Contribution of Women to National Development. I also got a commendation from an unusual source. Wole Soyinka had read my poems and written: "There is a good potential for you to excel beyond where my generation stopped. Keep it up!"

"You have been advertising yourself lately," he told me.

"How?" I asked.

"Forming clubs, joining NOW, and going to schools to preach rebellion to our young women! Now you are in the papers. Only God knows what you are selling yourself for," he complained.

"What's wrong in mobilizing young women to become responsible adults?" I asked.

Our women needed help and I was not daunted by his cheerless attitude to my work. I would continue to do my housework and make some effort to enter his heart. It was a difficult task but I did not want him to accuse me of being swollen headed because of being a lecturer.

5

THE LOVE OF POETRY

I discovered to my dismay about two years into marriage that my husband didn't like literature, and he had a special aversion to poetry. Immersed as he was in our customs and traveled as he had done, he was not a cultured man. Many who are not born with some talents learn them, but Nathan naturally lacked culture and did not want to acquire it. His exposure outside had been of no avail in this regard.

I would learn that in his secondary school, he was very proud of studying biology, chemistry, and zoology, the subjects that paved the way to medical school at the University of Ibadan, Ahmadu Bello University, or abroad. As was expected of every student at the time, Nathan had to study literature the first two years of secondary school. Of the ten subjects he took, that was the one he was least interested in. He always felt bored sitting for hours reading a novel based on fictitious characters and happenings. He preferred to read facts from newspapers than what he considered fiction. He loved the weekend papers, especially the *Lagos Weekend*, which many students clustered the sparse-spaced library to read. In it, he read about Wakabout's exploits. That was real stuff, he told himself. Wakabout relayed scandals from unexpected quarters—priests caught with members of their congregation making love, accused women bribing judges with their bodies, an eighteen-year old student sleeping with a seventy-year old sugar daddy, who died of heart attack while on top of her, and the like. Unlike most students of his age, he failed to understand that weekend papers were meant for entertainment and so were spiced with salacious stories that were either fiction or exaggerations of real happenings.

He found poetry a coded language that he never had the appetite to crack. It was very Greek to him, as he put it. So he scored a C in literature because the teacher was overgenerous to him, since he scored A in each of biology, chemistry, mathematics, and zoology. Already he saw himself as a thinker, a scientific brain who could solve theorems and successfully perform many experiments. He was always elated when he opened the mathematics set box and took any of the tools to approach his geometry and trigonometry. He loved a methodical approach that science espouses. A few of his friends called him "Formula," and he loved to hear that, since it confirmed to him his science orientation. You needed a formula to solve every problem, he contended. It did not occur to him that the so-called "guy's name" was vapid compared to his schoolmates with colorful names such as Kulele Kubanzi, Cotopaxi, Lobito, and Osei Tutu. Others loved the exotic, but he remained with the mundane and flat that gave no excitement.

I was not surprised because he had never been spontaneous or creative in behavior all the years I had known or lived with him. To him, sex is a night thing. He was never so moved as to pull me down by the sitting room sofa to make love. I wouldn't mind, as I sat stripped in the bathtub, if he removed his own clothes and came to fondle me. I wouldn't mind if in the sitting room he felt like a man and came to me. But he had his correct way of doing things; no change from the norm. He always wanted to be on top of me and never wanted any reversal of positions. When I once tried to have him down, he got up and asked me where I learnt my new style. He made me ashamed of my desire for change and killed my appetite for him. He became stale so early. He did not have the time to fantasize as literature appeared to him. If he had read those novels we secretly kept in our boxes out of sight of the reverend sisters, he would have been a more warm-blooded man. If only he had read *Do Not Go, My Love, We Two Together*, or *Jaguar Nana*, he would have been different. They would definitely have woken him from dormancy and made him a charger. He had read no romance novels, because they were literature that he despised. He embraced his rigid brand of science. After all, science deals with all sorts of experiments. Some experiments lead to new discoveries and unintended beneficial results. So, I cannot say it is because of science; it is because of his concept or brand of science.

Nathan felt relieved when, after coming out second in his class at the end of his second year, he was no longer required to read literature; no poetry. He felt that reading or writing poetry was a waste of time. He vigorously pursued his science option, on his way to doing something to lift society above itself. He envisioned himself as a Nigerian Pythagoras or Albert Einstein. As one of his Arts-option schoolmates taunted him when he visited us, he did not mix with people. "I hope you socialize a bit nowadays?" Garba asked him.

"Don't go into that," Nathan cautioned, like one who did not want his recluse past to be exposed.

"That's okay as long as you have time for Madam," Garba said, laughing.

"Madam, your husband has always dreamt of fame as a scientist," Garba continued; " I believe he must already be famous; after all, he is a doctor," he added.

I did not want to tell our marriage problems to Garba that I did not know before his unannounced visit. How he even got to our house, I did not know; but somebody who knew Nathan must have directed him. It then struck me that my husband had no friend, no best friend; in fact, there was no one close to him that I knew of. And yet he was not close to me. "Bye, Formula!" the visitor told him as he left. It was then that I learnt that he had "Formula" as a nickname. Nathan grimaced at hearing this name called. He felt exposed that I heard his school nickname. Our visitor brought out a side of Nathan I did not know. He must have wanted to be famous like the renowned scientists through learning. But if he had taken to medicine seeking fame, he must have soon discovered his practice to be more routine work than intellectual pursuit that would lead to any breakthrough discovery. Now he must be envying all those who had what he lacked—fame. He had never been comfortable beside anybody that he felt was popular, his wife or anyone else.

I still doubt whether Nathan ever loved me at any time, more so once he knew that I entered the University of Yerwa to study English, the very subject that he had no time for when in secondary school. To him, English, or call it literature, and myself had become synonymous concepts that appeared to have no relevance to his planned scientific life and fame.

I used to keep a diary until my long letter to Jo was intercepted. A diary made me look back and see what invisible order there might be in my life. I cherish memory a lot and memory of time past often helps to plan ahead. But I had to stop pouring my thoughts and experiences into a diary. I had to adjust by using only the medium of poetry to record my feelings and thoughts.

Nathan eavesdropped into what I was writing even before we started living together. Lord, thinking of the prolonged siege, I laugh at his folly. He did not read literature then and so did not know that not even God is watchful enough to catch a woman head-over-heels in love with somebody else. The woman who wants to meet the man she so much loves by all means will trick the Almighty to get to him! African tales tell us so. Will the woman not go to fetch firewood? Will she not go to the market to buy foodstuff? Will she not go out alone? The market is there to meet one's desire. And will the man himself, the guard, not go out and leave the woman some room to be alone? I thought of the East African tale in which a woman made a hole in her room through which she communicated and even made love with her lover. Nathan did not understand how futile it was to police a woman. And, of course, I was smoke that even a closed door could not contain from going out.

I had been humiliated beyond words in public, as I mentioned earlier. I had been summoned to a family assembly, before Nathan and I had married, to be indicted for writing Jo affectionately. Nathan had no shame and embarrassment stripping me in public and didn't mind if they stoned me unconscious to wake up and still be his wife! He read and translated my letter to the elders who were muted in their response, contrary to his highhanded expectations. The old men and women knew I had broken the traditional code of conduct for women who were betrothed to men. At a point, he abandoned reading the letter and summarized what I wrote, wishing circumstances had not separated Jo and me and hoping for a chance to meet in future. One old woman even asked him whether he wrote me and I didn't write him back, but her question was lost in indecisive grumbling. In any case, I was no thief. I was not yet then formally married to him, only engaged in a traditional way when his spying on me began. As he was determined to steal into me, I realized that I was going to fight back as a warrior ambushed in a desert plain with all the ingenuity and will power that I could muster.

I learnt to be more discreet with my letters. I would also record my feelings but in a more cryptic way to confuse the thief in the house. From thenceforth, he would see what I wanted him to see; except he broke into my room when I was out and he would do that often when he did not see anything to harass me about. I would not allow myself to be silenced in every way. I would not be entombed in the institution of marriage. Letters I continued to write to Jo and letters I continued to receive from him after he completed his sabbatical leave at the University of Yerwa and returned to the University of Lagos. My office became my address and the repository of a deluge of feelings.

For years Nathan knew that Jo had a Ph.D. from Columbia University in the United States of America and taught English/Literature and wrote poetry. He thought though that he was permanently at the University of Yerwa, where we had met during my studies. He had ransacked my bags and suitcases and found his poetry books. At first, he saw them as literature books and, worse for that matter, poetry. When he discovered that I also wrote poems, he became worried for reasons I could not easily fathom.

Soon he picked a quarrel for no reason. He saw a review of Jo's *Distant Routes* in a copy of *The Standard* that I had kept.

"I hope that your teacher and his poetry will not stop us from eating in this house," he said with exasperation.

He had been home, after abandoning his clinic, waiting for me to return from the Polytechnic at three in the afternoon to serve him lunch.

"What has my teacher got to do with your lunch?" I dared to ask.

"A lot. Every day if it is not that your teacher, Dr. Jonah Ogbe, it is the supervisor, or the Rector. Sometimes I wonder how many we are between your thighs," he muttered.

Since he closed his clinic and sat at home waiting for what next to do, he had been behaving rashly. Whatever I did exasperated him. He was sulking again. I knew that was the signal for complaints and senseless quarrel with me. Once his face was clouded dark, I expected the storm to break out immediately. And really, he flared up.

"Is it because I don't have a Ph.D. in English?" he asked thunderously.

I was surprised that a medical doctor in an enviable profession should feel inferior to a university teacher, whether he meant Jo, Professor Ayorinde, or the Rector. I thought he ought to be proud of his career, but he was definitely not from his utterances. There must be some secret disease gnawing ferociously at his mind and heart, which made him to flip over. He grabbed me by the throat and I was scared.

"Tell me, tell me," he shouted, as if he was talking to a deaf-anddumb person who was a distance away from him. He did not tell me what he wanted to know from me!

I pitied him. All of a sudden my thoughts went to his childhood story that Mama Goomsay had told many years back. My mother-in-law was in a jovial mood that day of our visit to her in Kwaton when Nathan was still running his clinic.

"Looking at you a doctor, nobody will know what you were as a child," she told him before me. After he left to see his friends around, my mother-in-law told me that, as a child, my husband used to wet his bed till very late for a boy. The habit stopped just before he entered the secondary school. I suppose some other boys with whom he grew up and also went to the same school knew about this, and he was very withdrawn from them for a long time. I believe he must have suffered silently over people's perception of him for lacking self-control. However, his mother told me that it was after his return from England that he had mustered enough courage to visit his age-mates still in town.

Jo was never my teacher as such because I did not take any of the courses that he taught. I attended only one event in which he gave a public lecture on "The Other Nigerian Literature" in which he discussed popular literature, especially from Onitsha, which really expressed the struggles and feelings of the common people. This Nigerian literature, he told the audience, was different from the works of Chinua Achebe, Wole Soyinka, and others that scholars and students write so much about. He wanted the subaltern literature taught side by side with the ivory tower writers' works.

Nathan would not believe me that Jo did not teach me at all. We met in circumstances that both of us still believe were destined. But Nathan would always nurse the belief that I was Jo's student, a lie. He must be thinking that Jo taught me all my four years at Yerwa and that my good results were a sort of favor from Jo for our relationship. It was beyond his reasoning that my hard work and whatever talent God has endowed me with earned me my Second Class Upper Division. But what he thought did not matter to me.

At first I did not expect that he would read my poems without my volunteering to read them to him or giving them to him to read. But that was what he judged right that I would not do at the time. If things changed, yes, I would give my poems to him to read if he expressed interest in reading. For now I would not share my inner feelings with him. I knew he would be stung by the feelings I expressed in those poems about relationships, which he would not find complimentary. I was only telling the truth of my condition. If I could not tell him how I felt, I told the whole truth to the muse. My muse was my confidant, from whom I hid nothing. I had become increasingly defiant, the more I felt tortured mentally and denied whatever would give me pleasure. I wrote "The Incubus" the day he laid down rules for me to obey. To him, I was no longer an adult but a child to be controlled by the parents' prescription.

"You have to submit to me your time-table at school. You spend too much time at school. You are always at school for one thing or the other," he rattled into the air.

My mind went back to my uncle, Magistrate Solomon Obida, and his orders, which his wife and I broke if we felt they were senseless.

"You can now only go to work the days that you teach, and once you are done, come home," he decreed.

"I have to meet students during my office hours. Will the students come to see me at home for their problems? Will the departmental meetings be held in this house?" I asked to make him understand that teaching was only a part of what a lecturer does at school, more so at The State Polytechnic, Barkin Ladi.

"And what of the instances when I will need to go to the library to check out books and references?"

To him, I had to use the notes I took as an undergraduate to teach my students. He did not believe in up-grading knowledge. And here was the man who felt Jo taught me and yet he wanted me to use the notes of the very person he did not want me to mention or think about.

I wanted him to see the irrationality of his reasoning by asking him a few more questions.

"And the meetings of the Academic Board should be held here at home? Seminars, workshops, discussion groups and drama rehearsals should take place in my kitchen because I have a loving husband who is afraid the men in the world will see his wife? Why don't you make me a *hajia* and keep me in purdah, go to the market, do all the shopping and all I need do is cook and spread out for you when it pleases you?"

He was perturbed at my anger. He was speechless for a while, then said: "The things you people learn in these institutions and in the name of poetry! You use dirty words without shame, a married woman?"

Nathan thought what was convenient or good for him was enough, irrespective of how the other person felt.

61

"I have told you my mind," he concluded, with the air of one who must be obeyed or whose sadism would be unleashed against a puny rebel.

I did not want to start a public uproar before the two children or for neighbors to witness. Dauda and Patrick were still elementary school and I took them to and from school daily. It would be wrong for us to do anything that would upset them emotionally. For the sake of peace, I declared a unilateral truce. I stayed at home or got special permission from his Highness, My Lord Husband, to go to my department on my so-called free days. I failed to move him to understand that in an institution of higher learning such as The State Polytechnic there was no free day for the lecturer, as I had to prepare for classes, grade papers, and try to write essays to publish lest I would perish career-wise. It was an entombment that I knew would not last long.

Though I was at home and he also at home, we did not laugh together. I gave so much of my time to reading and scribbling my sign language that he began to suspect that I was enjoying being buried alive. He might have reconsidered rescinding the grounding order he had slammed upon me. But he must have realized that I didn't care about his regulations and that I would always struggle to secure something to nourish me from his attempt to starve me.

But again, I failed to understand the man who would allow me no space to be myself. He now found the time when I left home to read my poems. And so when I came home one day, I met a severe face—not that it was unusual, but instead of sulking and keeping away from me, he flaunted his ugly side for me to see as if I didn't know that I had a tyrant for a husband.

He had got hold of my poetry manuscript. I had been emboldened to be defiant. I had been accused and condemned several times before for writing to, hearing from, and flirting with Dr. Jonah Ogbe or so many other men. I did not see what worse crime I would be accused of. I felt free to express my feelings on paper to my muse.

I had been working on *Plateau Life* for two years then. The table of contents had, among others, these revealing titles: "I am human," "I have secret freedom," "Smoke," "My parched throat," "Handbook of marriage," "Incubus love," "I know what it means to be buried alive," "Handbook of love," and "I, goddess." I did not attempt to hide anything, apart from the code name of Titi in place of Annie. I believe he got the message of these poems. I felt I had an absolute right to be myself, strip myself, in the privacy of my poems. If he read these poems, he was an intruder. He would see for himself that there was an alternative to him, a fact, which enraged him so much. He must have found out that both "Handbook" poems were meant to encourage our coming together, rather than drifting from each other. I wrote those two poems to encourage myself that however bad a marriage, from the onset something could be done to mend it. Love could be promoted consciously, if it was not there initially or naturally. I was ready to love him and be loved by him, but the effort had to be made. I wanted my children to have their parents together. Seeing those babies gradually becoming men was a great pleasure to me. I believe he was also pleased about the growth of the children. I suspected that most marriages had problems and separating was an easy way not to solve difficult problems. How I wish things would improve between Nathan and me!

I believe, however, that on reading them, some of the poems would have stung his manhood. He was angry but for the first time did not know how to express his rage. He knew that I was most unhappy with him over his attempt to entomb me but wanted to mend things for a good relationship. He also knew from these poems that I admired somebody else. Somebody else living very far away and I had not seen for so many years, but with whom I had maintained intermittent contact. He knew from my poems that Jo adored me, made me a goddess. How could the woman he lived with, his own wife, be this angelic Titi of the poems? He

63

must have queried his conscience and checked and re-checked his vision for what he could not see in me that Jo saw.

Now he started to string pieces together into a rope he wished would strangle me. But I would not submit myself to needless death. "I suspect all you women are like that and that is why many men do not like their wives to go to the university. See the way you befriended your supervisor till you got a Ph.D. and he had the audacity to come to ask me about you. Then it was the Rector writing you commendations. Of course, there is that man you say influenced you in Yerwa to get your first degree. From first degree to Ph.D. to work you just behave like a dog without an owner. I sometimes wonder if our parents did not make a mistake with this union. No one wants to marry everybody's sleep-mate."

I boiled with rage, held his shirt and wanted to fight him. But I would not give him the last word on this. "I guess you slept around in Edinburgh too to get your MBBS. And let me tell you, if you would not have respect for me the way you embarrass all those who help me achieve the heights I reach, God will punish you for it. You embarrassed that poor old man who was so kind to me, and you did the same to the Rector. If they were like you, I would not be where I am today. Ingrate, you can never understand what it means to be a good man."

"I am surprised you did not mention your undergraduate man, the poet, because you have no excuses left for that one. Go on; give excuses for your love poems to him. Go on, tell me how he is a good man since I am not a good man; tell me how good and manly he is. Go on; show some courage Dr. Annie the poet and playwright!"

"Dr. Goomsay, my loving husband, you are not a man and I repeat you are not a man. If you are, you will not be so petty as to tail your wife around and pry over her writings and letters. How many times do I go to your clinic to monitor which women you caress in the name of examination. I pity you, you need to grow up and stop being a teenager, Dr. Goomsay."

"You are playing with fire," he warned, brandishing his forefinger at me.

I expected him to explode like a volcano whose underbelly had been over-pressurized. I really wanted him to strike me and I was prepared for him this time. I had had my fill of his troubles and was going to fight back, really fight back. But he went away like a dog, his tail between his legs. I knew now how to handle him—call him a non-man.

He did not start a conversation, nor did I. Each of us tried to break the silence with the children. I noticed that he now asked the children how they fared at school. But when it came to their homework, he sent them to me. We did not eat together. I put his food on the table and left, and he would eat it before I was done with reading or caring for the children. We talked in monosyllables of "Yes" and "No" but no sustained exchange. I went to work as usual. He sat at home and plotted for the next political activity that would enhance his lobbying for a position. I was done with telling him to re-open his clinic, even if to be only a consultant in the vacant building. He was not aware of the self-waste of being trained as a physician with scholarship paid for with the people's money and his ending up as a political opportunity-seeker. And he was a very good physician that was needed by the people. Whatever our relationship had been, I admired his care, thoroughness, and patience when examining patients. The several times I had visited him in the defunct clinic, he touched me as an effective doctor and he must have saved many lives while in practice.

I was more than surprised several weeks later to see two poetry books—Byron's and Okot Bitek's—under his pillow in our bed. I did not want to interfere with his newfound passion, and so did not want him to know what I knew. After all, if he wanted to buy poetry books, he knew that I read, taught, and wrote poetry. He got hold of Jo's *Fixations* and *Distant Routes*. I knew he took the books from where I kept them. I did not protest over his raiding of my small library this time because I wanted him to read the books.

He now read poetry with such avidity that he did not hide what he was reading, but I paid him no attention. I looked forward to what effect poetry would have on him. Would poetry give him the sensitivity he lacked? Would poetry change him to a gentleman? What would the muse impart on him to make him charming? I waited for poetry to have its effects on him. He bought *The Advanced Oxford Dictionary* to check up the meaning of words he did not understand. I would have brought home the copy of the dictionary I had in the office if he had asked for it, but he acted as if I was either not around or irrelevant in this case. I could have saved him a little money, which he did not have anyway.

Unknown to him, I checked the books he read and now left unguardedly anywhere in the house. Maybe he wanted to let me know, without saying it, that he was reading poetry. He underlined words, ticked phrases and lines he must have enjoyed, and made comments by the sides. Reading Jo's poetry, he placed double question marks by traditional words that laced the poems. He did not see far or look far, because all of these terms were explained in the glossary. In any case, I believe he did not want to miss anything. He wanted to understand everything about me and about Jo whom he had not met outside the poems he wrote or I wrote for him and these books.

I pitied Nathan for what he was after. Was he, reading these poems, a dog following a scented trail, and to where? I knew he was torturing himself by reading Jo's poems and mine that he seized. If he did not tear up my poems, what service to him staring at the portrait of his victim and listening to her confessions? Even those poems I wrote to Jo were a response, and only a fool would fail to tell what these poems meant to Jo and me.

Nathan was hell-bent on knowing the secret magic of poetry that he felt Jo wielded over me like a wand. To him, Jo cast an irresistible spell over me, which he wanted to counteract with his knowledge of poetry. His thoughts ran one-way and lacked the subtlety of digression. Was he being true to his scientific training or what? I wished him the best of luck in his pursuit. He also wanted to learn how to write poetry. I think he wanted to know about my past, especially the years of our engagement when he was in Britain and did not bother to write me. Of course, after his reply to my letter and I wrote him twice again without a reply from him, I held back.

He must have learned some things about me from these poems that he did not yet know. That would have bothered him a lot, living with me as a stranger after many years of marriage. And he was trying to recreate in his narrow mind a big picture of Jo whom he had never met, whose photo I believe he had not seen unless from his books, but who had now become the third adult in his home.

6

IN BED WITH TWO MEN

It started when I was a final year student at the University of Yerwa. The first time Jo and I went out, we ended up passing the night together. We talked, played, and laughed all night. Don't jump to hurl insults at me, as if I was too easy to get. No, you could only do that when you were not in my shoes. If you were, you would understand my action. I had been in the university for four years and had had no boyfriend as such. Debra and I were friendly with our course mates, but there had been no intimacy in any of the cases. So, I knew very well how to hold back. I had consciously kept away from any intimacy until I could not help it.

We had both waited for the outing for many months and appeared to have emotionally surrendered ourselves to each other long before the date. But that was after a long battle that I had to fight within. I believe Jo went through the same battle on his part. From the beginning, none of us pretended about how we felt for each other. But that was the easy part—liking somebody might not be the same as getting involved emotionally with the person. Later, after the battles of confused right thing to do, we must have been swept away emotionally. Once we got involved, we felt no qualms over our relationship, and so did not hold back from the other. Let busybodies go to hell, we felt.

We had met under very inauspicious circumstances. When I think of that first meeting, I feel ashamed of myself. But civil as Jo was, he always told me when I reminded him of it that it was good for one to show one's displeasure outwardly, rather than be consumed within by ill feelings.

"Spit out bitterness from your system rather than be infected by a vile contagion," he told me afterwards.

The day we first met remains vivid in my memory. I had gone to the secretary's office. I can't even recollect the very reason for my going there, but I was angry because of something. Yes, I now remember. The typist I had paid a fortune to type my long essay had messed it up. I had secured the typist's services through the secretary to whom he had handed over what was supposed to be the finished work. Enraged that the sixmonth labor that I had invested so much money and time on was badly typed, Jo entered amidst the altercations between the secretary and me. I had seen him before from a distance and knew he was new in the department. However, I did not know whether he was a visiting or permanent lecturer. In more than three years I had been here, lecturers had come and gone, some visiting and some permanent ones resigning and taking up new jobs elsewhere. A few girls had talked about him in the girls' hostel but in vague terms. None knew him well. He was a stranger.

Now in the department office, I could see his eyes questioning me as to why I should be angry over what could be remedied in a simple discussion. There would always be something in his eyes that I always liked to look to for inspiration or guidance. A vision always telling me something I needed to know that I had either not or ignored.

"Hi!" he greeted me.

"Good afternoon," I answered.

"What's wrong? You don't have to squeeze your face," he asked and counseled me, his words definitely aimed at me and not the secretary.

"Yes," I replied impulsively.

I did not know what I was saying "Yes" to.

The secretary had watched for a minute or so as we greeted and stared at one another. He felt he had to introduce us to each other. He didn't, I believe, want to remain in the crossfire.

"Dr. Ogbe, this is one of our final-year students, Anna Dosang. And Miss Dosang, this is our visiting senior lecturer, Dr. Jonah Ogbe."

We simultaneously stretched out our hands for a handshake. His hand was warm, friendly, and alluring; his grip gentle but firm. He held my hand and looked into my eyes or face, saying "Nice to meet you."

"Nice to meet you too," I responded.

Dr. Ogbe looked young to have had a doctoral degree and be a senior lecturer. I knew the Ph.D. holders in the department and elsewhere in the university looked much older. He was of medium height, neither tall nor short. He carried glittering eyes and a face exuding warmth. He was agile and confident in his strides. I would know so much of him that though we did not live together, we would be each other's most familiar.

It is true that once you know somebody or something, you begin to notice him or it more often. From then on, we would meet randomly but frequently. We often met on the corridor and exchanged smiles, at first without uttering a word; and later giving a quick nod or wave of the right hand. Signs in these circumstances communicated much more than we were too coy to air.

69

I did not take any of the three courses that he was teaching. I had taken them in earlier semesters and had made A's in all three. I would tell him this much later, and it gladdened him immensely and reinforced the very high regard he had for me. Somehow, we gravitated to each other almost every weekday in the campus. I felt he wanted to talk to me or with me as I was burning for the same. The opportunity or relief came sooner than I expected. One Friday afternoon we met again on the corridor; he was about leaving his office, perhaps for the day. Even before we repeated our now familiar ritual of nodding or waving hand, he beckoned on me. I went to him.

"Annie, if you have a little time, can we talk?"

"Yes," I replied with a smile.

He smiled back. The hide-and-seek game was over. He abandoned wherever he was about going and stepped back into his office, after me. On Fridays, lectures were suspended between noon and four to allow Muslims go to the mosque for worship. Of course, the weekend spirit already gripped everybody and Muslims and non-Muslims alike cashed on the four-hour break to disappear from the office. Neither students nor lecturers returned for lectures or serious work that day. The weekend had begun.

"Sit down, Annie," he said, pointing to a chair opposite his across the big desk.

The way he called my name appeared special from the very first day we were introduced to each other. His voice soft, endearing, and so uniquely masculine it can be picked from a market of voices.

The office had several art works hanging on the wall. His was a spacious room for an office. A Benin FESTAC queen mother's headpiece adorned one side of the room. Also on the wall an Ekpe masquerade woven on a raffia mat. There was also a bow zither or musical instrument of the sort that was itself a beautiful artwork. The bookshelves were filled.

"Have you read all these books?" I asked.

70

"They are not all mine but I have read many," he replied. He was occupying Dr. Yusuf Abba's office. Dr. Abba had taken leave of absence after accepting a political appointment from the Borno State Government. My eyes fell on Dr. Ogbe's name on the middle shelf. I rose to get a closer look at two books with his name.

"I didn't know you were an author," I told him. "A beginner author. Just two books of poems." "An author is an author," I told him.

He was fairly shy and didn't want to be praised for his books of poems.

"Some day students will be studying you. What do you think of that prospect?" I asked.

"Hopefully, they'll enjoy my work," he said.

"They'll know your ideas and feelings," I added. "And that scares me," he put in briskly.

I did not want to ask why he would feel scared that students read him; but I supposed in a poem, by registering one's private feelings, one strips before the reader. I would later understand very well why it would be a scaring experience. "Do you read or write poetry?" he asked me. "Yes, of course. I have to read poetry to pass my literature exams. But Doctor, I like poetry. I try to scribble some lines now and then, but I don't know whether what I write is poetry or doggerel."

"Happy to meet you, Poetess Annie," he said and offered his hand to me.

I took his hand. As we shook hands, I thought of my new title, Poetess Annie.

"By the way, I am Jo. Don't call me Doctor. Call me by my name," he told me.

"You are a lecturer and I can't call you by your first name. Let me call you Doctor Ogbe," I suggested.

71

"No. Call me Jo, at least when only we two are together."

"Okay. Only when we are together alone."

We were already having a pact that expected us to be together alone and to call each other familiar names.

He brought out of his desk's drawer a copy of his *Mountain Skies* and autographed it for me. "For Annie: with very warm regards" and signed and dated it February 16, 1982. I felt honored, moved, and spellbound. I had met a published poet in person. I had read English and American literatures and all the authors died a long time ago. The African authors I had read were living, but were so far away. I couldn't imagine talking with Chinua Achebe, J.P. Clark, or Wole Soyinka and having a copy of their work personally signed for me.

We looked at each other. He realized that he had asked me in. Maybe he saw my eyes questioning why or what he wanted to see me for.

"Annie, I just wanted to chat with you. There is nothing special or specific to talk about. We see each other very often and I just wanted to know you more."

"No problem. Where have you come from?" I asked.

I had known from student gossip contradictory information about him, but wanted him to introduce himself fully to me. I would now know whether or not he had just come back from the United States or he was on sabbatical from the University of Ibadan or Lagos.

"I am on sabbatical leave from the University of Lagos, Unilag. I should have come earlier, but our calendar had been disrupted with a local strike; hence I came in this January. This means I will stay through December to have a full academic year here before going back," he explained.

"You are welcome to The University of Yerwa," I told him, as if I was the representative of the university.

He attended Columbia University where he took an M.FA. in creative writing and a Ph.D. in English.

"University of Lagos sponsored me, and I went back five years ago to teach there."

Pay back what he owed, I thought. That was responsible of him to return. I had heard of many lecturers, who got either Government or University scholarships and refused to return to fulfill the terms of their contracts when they were done with their studies. There was no way of bringing home Government- or University-sponsored scholars from abroad against their will, so those who came back to pay their dues should be lauded for their sense of responsibility.

"Nice that you returned to serve your sponsors," I told him.

"It was my duty," he replied.

"Not all people take duty seriously. I am happy you went back to Lagos and that's why you are able to be here in Yerwa now," I said.

"Okay. Thanks for thanking me for doing my duty. In any case, I have completed the mandated four years and could now leave if I wanted to."

Would he like to remain in Yerwa after his sabbatical leave? This university certainly needed more lecturers.

"I will go back to Lagos in December. I wanted to experience this part of the country and I hope to have a surfeit of it before I go back." I didn't want to ask him about his home in Nigeria. I could tell he was a Southerner. If nothing else, his choice of clothes—no caftan, no *baba riga* robes, only shirts and trousers, and an occasional *adire* on top of trousers. Was he not Yoruba from his dress and his workplace? I asked myself.

"Guess my place of birth," he challenged me.

I was startled by his declaration, as it seemed he read my mind and answered my silent question. I was not sure and did not want to make a fool of myself. He could be from anywhere in the South. After all, the educated men from there dressed casually. I shook my head to signify that I did not know for sure where he came from.

"I am from Warri, Bendel State," he told me.

73

I was not too surprised about where he came from even though I would not have guessed it right.

"And you, Annie, must be from Benue-Plateau from your name?"

"Yes," I answered. "From the Plateau side."

"I guessed as much."

"Why?"

"Am I not a Nigerian? I know people and places."

Later I was to know that he attended Federal Government College, Afikpo, where he met young men and women from all over the country. In his days, students were picked from every local government in the country and the schools were truly "Unity Colleges." After graduating from the University of Lagos, Dr. Ogbe taught at Federal Government College, Afikpo, where he could have taught more Nigerians of diverse ethnic backgrounds.

We talked about our department of English, Yerwa, and about Benue-Plateau and Bendel States.

"What about your long essay?" he asked.

"It's been re-typed," I told him.

"I am glad it's now done to your satisfaction," he told me. I did not want to remember my anger the day we met in the secretary's office, the day I could not control my rage. I might have made the same point without boiling over. But that was gone.

That first time we sat to chat in his office, we both forgot about time. About three hours had passed in a flash.

That night in my room in the hostel, I would write my first poem in a very long while. And once it came out, I started writing poetry more regularly. It was as if he had removed a blockage to allow a free-flow of my feelings. Before I left the office, my heart was beating fast and loud before his eyes, smiles, and hand. He was also flushed with emotions. From then on, I stopped by his office on Fridays for our now regular chats.

You don't have to tell the antelope what the grassland is; it is its abode. I am a woman, and about to graduate from the university. At twenty-three, I was big enough to be a mother. We senior girls talked about men and love in and out of the hostel. I therefore knew that Jo admired me from his looks and compliments.

"You look exquisite!"

"You are gorgeous!"

"You are angelic!"

"Goddess of the plateau!"

The compliments had gradually elevated me to a divine state. I reciprocated, though I couldn't match his epithets.

"Prince of Words!"

"My muse!"

I learnt a lot from him and he told me that he also learnt so much from me. He told me that I was more his muse than he was my muse. I didn't want to contest that with him, since I believed that that would show someday.

I started to look up to Friday as to a feast from which I always walked away fulfilled and yet desiring for more. It was a communion for which I was ready to sacrifice other activities with my friends. When they wanted to go to town for shopping, I gave them some excuses to stay in the campus and spend time with Dr. Ogbe in his office. At the beginning I spent many sleepless hours at night reflecting on what I was putting myself into. Was this mere chatting or love? If it were love, would it not complicate our lives? How could I be betrothed and not tell him? How would I handle the situation if it went too far? But I liked his cheerfulness, warmth, and intellectual acumen. I was gradually putting caution aside. I needed his company as perhaps he needed mine.

The Friday before my final examinations started, Jo proposed that after I was done we should go out for dinner in town. I couldn't refuse such an invitation, as I was already crazy to be with him whenever and wherever possible. He must have understood psychology very well because he knew how to inspire without distracting me from my school's work. And that made me go through more sleepless hours at night. Did he like me or not? Was he fighting within himself too on whether to get close or not? I was very touched by his card wishing me success in the exams. It was a beautiful flower opening up bright red, a rose. It was big and of very high quality.

I did not receive any letter or card from Nathan who wrote four months earlier that he would be visiting home; mind you, home and not me, by June ending. I wrote him that I would be taking my final exams then. It was coincidence that his visit fell at the same time as my final exams. There was neither a letter nor a card from him, my betrothed! I would have expected a serious suitor or fiance to tell me that he would visit me in school. Don't think that I am trying to justify my liaison with Dr. Ogbe, no.

I now had more than a personal reason in Dr. Ogbe to perform very well in the examinations. I was confident that he would be very proud of my performance and would admire me even more. I would not let myself down before someone who liked me so much as to care that I performed well. His wishes gave me the inspiration I needed to excel more than I had even imagined.

After the examinations, which ended for me on Friday at noon, we met at six in his office from where we walked to his navy blue Honda Accord car. I had tried to take a nap in the afternoon, but the excitement of the outing that evening prevented me from falling asleep. Did I think I was going to oversleep and miss the date? No, I was just restless. I had gone to bathe three times within two hours! Though it was the season of intense heat and dust, what dirt was I washing away from my body? I was barely dry before I went to the bathroom again. I changed dresses as many times. I first tried on my traditional evening attire that fitted me well; but I took it off and wore a gown. I did not need a seductive evening dress to go out for the first time with a man that I was confused about. Finally, I settled on a pair of blue jeans and a white T-shirt. I wanted to be simple, smart and comfortable. I felt the other dresses were too formal—after all, I was not going to church or an interview. I wanted to be casual and yet decent, hence I settled on what I wore.

I knew that my roommate must have wondered what I was up to that made me look for so much perfection. But a junior student, Patricia Okoh politely kept quiet, though she kept on looking at me. I believe she knew that I was going out to see somebody I liked so much. For two years she had shared the room with me, I had not once behaved this way. A few times, she had accompanied me to the market or to town. This time I did not tell her where I was going or whom I was going to meet. This day should have intrigued her to suspect I was falling in love or already in love. I hardly used make-up. I put on a Vaseline lip balm and sprayed a Timeless Avon perfume over my body. I felt fresh and comfortable. Only when I was about to step out of the room did Patricia give me a broad smile and a nod. I took her gestures to be signs of approval of my dress and simple make-up.

Both of us were prompt with the tryst. Dr. Ogbe opened my side door, held it while I went in, and closed it after I was seated. He then went round to his driver's side. Before he started the car, he told me that he hoped I wouldn't mind going to the Chinese restaurant in town.

"That's fine with me," I told him.

"I wanted to be sure," he said.

The drive was leisurely. Jo took the Yobe Bridge Road that went through the GRA part of town and avoided the crowded Hospital Road. It was evening though and most Muslims must have been at home waiting for the evening prayers before dinner. We turned into Kashim Ibrahim Avenue and took a left at Bank Road. Within twenty minutes we were at our destination.

The Chinese restaurant was undoubtedly the most luxurious eatingplace in town. I had never entered it before then, but a few of my classmates, who did, talked much about it. It was simply called "Jade Garden." It was rugged red and lit red with chandeliers. The atmosphere was plush, to say the least. The walls were emblazoned with Chinese art. There were tiny animal motifs, and one could see dragons, rats, snakes, if one drew very close to the wall. I knew the Chinese assigned each year to a creature and wondered what animal represented the year we were in.

We waited behind a group to be seated, and when it came to our turn we were led to a table for two. We placed an order for a mixture of chicken and shrimp and an assortment of Chinese vegetables. Every order came with a bowl of white rice. We ordered a medium bottle of red wine that should give each of us two full glasses. The appetizer soup was hot and highly palatable. The main dish itself took some time to come, which we didn't mind anyway because we were busy talking. The meal itself was the greatest treat I had had outside. I had a very sharp appetite that night and ate voraciously, as Jo did amidst conversation.

We were no longer lecturer and student, just two human beings that liked each other. At table, as had been in his office all the Fridays, I didn't ask him whether he was married or not. He wore no ring, but I suspected that he might be already married. Would the poet not find it too conventional to wear a ring? I asked myself. He did not ask me either whether I was married or not. I did not volunteer to him that I had a traditional obligation either. Many of us female students leaving the university were already married or engaged like me. Usually, men wanted to commit the girls before they left for national service and got exposed to many men they could choose from for partners. Men were very cunning in this. "Catch them early before they are overexposed," they told themselves. They wanted to be experienced, but not their wives!   We must have both felt that we were friends already, and whatever earlier commitments we made, we were going to remain friends. Someday, I would tell him my status as I felt he would tell me his. We were free, though tethered to a post, I suspected. Jo once told me about a creature, during a period of famine, that carried a dead fly—it was hungry but would not eat a dead thing, but could not throw it away because nobody threw away available meat in days of famine! The folk tale might appear unrelated to us, but I thought it aptly described our different circumstances.

Jo had brought along a camera—it appeared he always left it in his car and he took it as we came down earlier.

"You never know when a camera will be of use," he had said.

He took pictures of me several times. I also snapped pictures of him. We asked a chef to take both of us, and he had a wide smile after snapping both of us. Perhaps he was wondering whether we were newly wed or engaged. We talked, held each other's hands, fed each other, and smiled copiously at ourselves. I did not want that night to end. We were the last customers to leave the restaurant. The chefs and others were very polite but must have wanted us to leave so that they could close for the night. It was already very late—close to midnight!

Outside the restaurant and beside the car, we hugged. I could feel in my breasts his body burning with tenderness and desire. I had my first adult kiss with him. All the so-called kisses earlier were shallow and mere lip-service gestures to love. This was different, deep and unique. I was wet with emotions. My body tingled with excitement and I was entering a state of possessed excitement, but I held my own. Did we as girls not advise each other not to yield to a man, however much we love him, during the first outing? Was I not engaged and he married, and what would this friendship really lead to? I was excited and confused. Maybe nothing would come out of this friendship, but something that would fizzle out with time. After all, I would leave in a few weeks, and he would be back in faraway Lagos by December.

After I entered the car and he was about to start the engine, he asked, if I didn't mind, whether we could still go out.

"We are already out," I teased him.

"I mean stay out longer," he explained, as if I did not get the import of his suggestion.

I was ready to stay out longer with him. We drove aimlessly in town for about thirty minutes before his mind settled on where to go. He might be thinking of taking me to know his place, but I was not sure. All along my heart beat fast. I was unusually excited and did not care wherever he took me to. My lighthearted defense had already crumbled. When he turned towards Shehu Laminu Way, I knew we were heading for his apartment, since he had described where he lived to me. The colonial officers had planned the Government Reservation Area for their quiet living. The houses were spaced out and *neem* trees lined both sides of the road. Both of us were quiet for about several minutes, as we knew where he was going. Then he said, "I hope you don't mind knowing my place."

"But we must be already close," I told him.

"Yes, I apologize," he said. "No, it's fine with me," I assured him.

I was happy he did not choose a hotel for our first outing. I was relaxed and yet anxious because of my feelings. I knew many men took female students to hotels in town and would not like it for the first outing, though I wouldn't mind wherever my man took me to once we became intimate in every sense of a relationship. It was already very late and it might be he wanted us to talk before taking me back to the campus. We were too full to take any drink or food.

He had a three-bedroom bungalow that was sparsely furnished but cluttered with books and magazines. I was not surprised at the so many books, magazines, and sheets of paper on tables and chairs. I did not expect less of a writer's home. He had given one of his bedrooms to Samuel, who was newly employed by Ramat Polytechnic. They were not related but Samuel was related to one of his friends in Lagos and needed space. He might have wanted somebody to share the chores with him too.

Samuel had not yet gone to bed that late. He was listening to music. Jo brought out drinks because, as he put it, he had to welcome me to his home. Of course, we were already too full to drink more.

Samuel soon left the sitting room for us, telling us that he was going to a neighbor's house. The neighbor was his friend who taught in Yerwa Government College. He went to his room, a little removed from two other bedrooms, picked his keys, I believe, and left. Once left alone, we knew we were stuck with each other for the night.

There are experiences that cannot be fully described. I fought a battle over what my feelings were prepared for but my head wanted to resist. The resistance was too feeble to hold back the waves of feelings that overwhelmed me. There are no words to express moments of fulfillment. I wish I could fully convey joy and bliss. I experienced them for the first time, and I knew the difference they made on me. After sitting for a while listening to music, we played WHOT cards. I had seen the cards on the table and I asked that we play. It took us some time; it must have been up to an hour and a half before we stopped playing. We had the game even at three-three. We knew he had to take me back to the campus or go to bed together there. Then we talked, laughed, and played as we expected the inevitable. We talked about our childhood, upbringing, and beginnings. We were opening ourselves to each other, a preamble to the ultimate communion. We kissed again, and the great moment came. He held my hand to raise me from the chair and led me to his bedroom. We sat for a moment, feeling each other's heartbeat. We stripped. After clasping each other for moments, we were breathing fast with desire. When he entered me, it was so tenderly, our bodies warm and moist. I felt an electric charge as we floated downstream, as if in a dugout for two in a climactic crash into a sea of pleasurable grunts. Each time we came, it was so lovely—we cried out and burst into meaningless chants. I wanted to rest and dance at the same time; he wanted more. What a communion!

We did not realize how fast time had gone and did not know it was about dawn. When we heard the sound of cars, we looked at the clock on the wall to find that it was already five-fifteen. When a few cocks crowed, we knew he had to take me back to school. I was traveling home that morning. We had embraced and knew that we were beginning to travel a long road.

He dropped me by the hostel just before six o'clock. I had sent a message to my mother that I was coming that day and she would expect me. If I had not sent word to her, I would have just gone to bed, slept, and relaxed with the aftertaste of the previous night. I took a warm bath, dressed, and rested a bit before setting out for the motor park to catch a taxi to Bukuru.

Bukuru was cold. The area had two cold seasons, one during the harmattan and the other during the raining season. The daily afternoon thunderstorms of the wet season had begun. It was early July. Once it rained, at night you had to bundle up with thick clothes so as not to catch cold or pneumonia. But I was used to that, and I expected cool weather. Nathan Goomsay did not provide any heat either. You could tell when a man looked forward to meeting or having a woman he loved. You could feel the heat from a distance. There was no fire of anticipation in Nathan. I didn't have any for him either.

I went to see him. Even though my parents had sent word to him that I was coming that day, he did not come to wait for me in Bukuru. I had to go and see him in his Kwaton. His parents, especially his mother, were warmer towards me than he was. That was, after we had not seen each other for two years. His last visit was a disaster and I had felt that time would transform the lukewarm relationship we had into something much warmer.

Yes, I slept with him; but it was as if his heart was not there with me. And, of course, mine was elsewhere. In Yerwa my heart was for sure.

After the previous night in which stars exploded in my head and I was borne downstream in that dugout for two that crashed into a sea of pleasure, the night in Kwaton was damp and I was eager to escape from it. By the following day, I saw emptiness in my life that Nathan could not fill. There was something special missing in me, and he made no attempt to provide it anyway. Why did he come? I asked myself. He did not seem to have come because of me. Did he come to parade himself before Kwaton and Nang people as a medical student in Britain, a physician in the making? He still had a year left to complete his studies. He was unreadable. I learnt from others that he had only five days left for him to go back to Britain. I excused myself that I had to be back in Yerwa for my results. He didn't seem to care.

Two days later I was back in Yerwa, back to Dr. Ogbe. My results were expected in a week, after which I would be posted for the national service. That week would remain indelible in my memory for the time I spent with Dr. Ogbe. The university was about closing for the long vacation. Examinations were already completed. The lecturers were grading papers, they were eager to submit results and to begin their vacation travels. Students were leaving for home, though many final-year ones stayed behind to check their results that would soon be published. We took a trip to Mubi just to get out of town and feel free with each other. Mubi was cool, but not the dampness of Bukuru and Kwaton that I had fled from. We had time to take walks in the big complex of State Government Hotel, where we stayed. We read poems to each other and practiced writing a poem together. He started with a line and I followed with my line until we had a twenty-four-line poem titled "Partners." We sat by huge tall trees to enjoy outdoor air. In the late afternoon, we drove to the Cameroon border and admired the scenery of hills and grassland vegetation. At a frontier town called Banki, we sat down at a bar and drank *trois trois*, the good-tasting beer that was not then available in Nigeria.

We wanted to spend more time together, but we just had to come back for me to know my posting for the national service. When we returned to Yerwa, the results were already published. I suspected that Jo might have seen mine, but did not tell me about it. I made a Second Class Upper Division. Jo congratulated me profusely and I could feel that he was very proud of me.

I could not stay behind when the hostels were closed. I had to go to Kano for the national service orientation. I did not care whether Nathan was still in Kwaton or gone back to Edinburgh. Since he had only one year left in his studies, I knew I had to make a choice, a hard one. A choice as to whether I should actually *make* a choice, or let things go the way of traditional customs. Must I follow duty or desire? Could I have both? Were both duty and desire not meant to fuse in a relationship? Magistrate Solomon Obida, by virtue of being my maternal uncle and whose blessing was thus most needed, had thrown his weight behind the engagement. Nathan must have met him during his visit.

IN SEARCH OF MY HEART'S DESIRE

The moment Annie left for national service, I was thrown into a suffocating void. My sabbatical year was running out, but I still had some time left. She wrote often as soon as she got to the orientation camp, but all of a sudden when she was supposed to be out of the camp, there was no correspondence from her. She last wrote as they were about to be posted to their workplaces in the State. She wrote two to three letters a week before this time. What now could have happened that stopped her from writing just one letter in a week, not even the two or three I was getting used to? Something must have happened to stop her from writing, a situation that I suspected she could not control. All I wanted to do was to get out and look for her. It was a difficult task that I set for myself. I was a hundred and ten percent sure that as I looked for her, so too would she be anxious to get in touch with me.

I had no inkling of where she was in Kano, a very large state that had common borders not only with four other states but also with the countries of Chad and Niger. Annie might be inside Kano, the capital city, or anywhere in the state. I knew she would teach, since the state was short of all categories of teachers and especially of English. In fact, during the later stage of the orientation for the national service, she had sent a note to me that they were far gone in the exercise and would be sent at the end to different parts of the state. She liked the exercises, especially the paramilitary aspects of rope climbing, jogging, and marching. She also said that she liked the camaraderie, but she missed me, as she knew I too missed her. That long period of silence when I did not hear anything from her after they had been posted was for me like going through hell. I started to make inquiries from those I felt might know about the national service headquarters in Kano. I got to know that working there was a certain Henry Okotie, who came from my area. With Samuel at the steering, we took off one early Wednesday morning for Kano in search of Annie by way of the office of the National Youth Service Corps. We met Mr. Okotie, who looked familiar to me and he told me I also looked familiar—we might have met in one of the innumerable social gatherings we used to hold during vacation times many years ago. After all, he came from Effurun that had grown to join Warri and the two towns were now called Effurun-Warri.

After telling him my mission, he asked for files of the postings to be brought and saw that Annie was posted to Government Teachers' College, Bichi. Bichi was some two and a half hours drive from the city of Kano, and that was a short distance bearing in mind that we had already driven seven hours from Yerwa. Samuel and I left Kano at about one o'clock in the afternoon for Bichi.

I had observed the diminishing grassland as we traveled from Yerwa to Kano, but driving northwards to Bichi exposed me to the true meaning of the Sahel. The grass was browner than anything I had ever seen in the dry season elsewhere. The endless plain was more sand than grass, and plants in sight were stunted, thin, and starved of moisture. I wondered how people survived in that environment that could barely sustain animals and plants. The cattle herdsmen and their animals were gaunt. A sandstorm blurred visibility and showered everybody with dust. Being inside the car was of no use as the dust had its subtle way of penetrating closed windows. The road, anyway, was well maintained; the traffic very low compared to roads south of the city going to Zaria and Kaduna.

With curiosity and a sense of wonderment, we arrived in Bichi. A fairly small town, the signposts directing to Government Teachers' College were many and we arrived there without asking anybody for its location. At the school, I asked for Anna Dosang and learnt that she did not show up and was believed to have gone elsewhere. I took a picture of the school, where Annie should have been but was not.

Leaving Bichi, we headed straight back to Yerwa. Samuel had to go to work the following day since he took only one day off, and I had to teach too. I would wait till Annie wrote, as I surely felt she would. The journey to Kano and Bichi intensified my search for Annie. I spent a day and a night, covering about two thousand miles. We drove all night to arrive in Yerwa at dawn on Thursday. I did not see the trip as futile. Nothing I did for the sake of Annie could be futile. I had gone in search of my heart's content.

The void expanded, deepened, and suffocated me the more. I was mum in the house. Maria who had come from Lagos to visit me that weekend must have noticed my strange mood, but did not ask me whether anything was wrong or not before she returned. She might have thought that I was tired of being in Yerwa that was so far away from Lagos. With the extreme weather of very hot and very cold seasons, how would those used to Lagos not feel uncomfortable in Yerwa? With the swarms of flies all year round, how would one get used to Yerwa? But my cheerless mood had nothing to do with extreme weather or flies.

I did not eat with the same relish the very foods that I used to devour—my plates had a lot of leftovers. I went to bed much earlier and woke several times in the night, tossing sleeplessly. I tried to write, but no inspiration came. I tried many games. I chanted words I had read from a copy of *The Rosicrucian Digest* to bring Annie to me. I tried to conjure her into my presence, was able to emblazon her image in the air, but the substance could not be found.

It was a matter of time, I believed, for Annie and me to hear from each other or even meet. I knew we were searching from different directions. During this time of waiting, after the journey to Kano and Bichi, I could write only one poem and it was meant to cheer me up. The mental work was bearing some fruit at least.

THE PROBLEM OF FILLING AND REFILLING

(written after a trip to Bichi, Kano)

We always look for spaces to fill: a school
with pupils, a blank sheet with words a
register with names, a catalogue with titles,
humanity with births and deaths.

We fill time with a network of dreams, silence
with ruminations, inexhaustible habits that
bend over us to fix their schedules.

And after the filling, we clear the places,
bulldozers and hands at our disposal: make a
road for our desires, clear the air to fly for a
full vision of our held-back paradise. Then we
leave those spaces to be refilled, empty gas
cylinders, stalls in the market.
The sun's filled with the sweat and smell of clothes.

I am the sufferer, half-smothered by desires; I
have filled an empty journey with meaning.

Continuing to suffocate in the void of Annie's absence, I contemplated going to Nang, her birthplace. Could Annie have gone to Bukuru, where she spent her vacations with her uncle or to Nang to be with her parents? She had told me that her parents were contemplating moving from Nang to Bukuru, since the old village did not hold much for people to

89

do for a living. Were her parents still in Nang or have they relocated to Bukuru? Was she well or what was the problem?

Whether my anxiety over Annie or something else was the cause, I could not tell. My hemorrhoids worsened. I have had hemorrhoids for a long time, and they flared once in a while in a pattern I could not determine. I shat blood for two days. By the third day, I went to the University Clinic. After my description of the pain, protruding rear end, and dripping blood, the doctor asked me to take off my trousers, lie on a table, and pull down my underwear, which I did. He then put on gloves and examined my rear end. It was swift.

"Your case is messy," the consultant told me in what I considered to be non-clinical jargon.

"You need immediate surgery, if the hemorrhoids are not to cause you further problems. You run the risk of blood infection," he added.   He referred me to the University Teaching Hospital for specialist attention. Only general medical care was available at the University Clinic. The University Teaching Hospital had specialists and surgeons who took care of serious cases.

"How soon will this surgery take place?" I asked.

"I told you that it is critical; that is, it needs to be worked on immediately. It's the surgeon at the Teaching Hospital that will book you for the nearest available date. My job is to report the urgency of your condition," he answered.

The doctor had pronounced. I obliged to his order for immediate surgery. It was Thursday afternoon and he sent me to a surgeon in the hospital to book an appointment. He said that he was going to call him and see whether it could be done on Monday. The point reached me clearly that my condition was serious and urgent.

I prepared myself for the surgery. Desisting from eating solid foods the day before, I had to take pap or custard three times that day. The surgeon also gave me a purgative drug to clear my stomach. I was forbidden from taking even water after midnight of the eve of the surgery. After being stripped and re-clothed with a patient's pajamas uniform, I was wheeled in a bed between two automatic doors into the operating room. I saw nurses and doctors waiting eagerly for me. I had been naïve about what theaters were. Taking my cue from literature, I had expected a central place where the surgery would take place and surrounding seats for the nurses and other attendants. Was this an amphitheater? It was a fairly big room by hospital standard, well lit with fluorescence. The chief surgeon and his attendant doctors and nurses were masked with their eyes showing in a light green overall.

"How do you feel?" the lead surgeon asked me.

"Fine!" I replied.

"Do you feel any pain anywhere?"

"No!"

"Did you have a good sleep last night?"

I knew they were kneading me on to a state of unconsciousness. If I was anxious and slept little the previous night, did they expect me to tell them my shame? Very soon, I surmised, they would ask me about my dreams last night. In one of the many dreams, Annie visited in the company of a group of youth service ladies to see me in my office! The other ladies were asking her "Who is this?" when I woke. Neither she nor I spoke.

"Everything is set and you'll be fine," the lead surgeon assured me.

"Thank you," I replied.

"We'll try to send you to sleep and by the time you wake, everything should be done. You'll be fine."

At that moment, they placed some type of air mask in my face and asked me to inhale. After inhaling what was held before me, I wandered within a few minutes into an unconscious state.

I woke to a list of don'ts. That first week after the surgery was the most excruciating in my life. I took only watery foods. Relieving myself in the toilet was so painful that I held back till it was absolutely necessary to do so. I was to stay in the hospital for five days.

"You'll feel the pain in one way or another for up to six months. There will be pain even after the wound has healed. That's normal," the surgeon told me.

"Thank you" was all I could say to him.

"You have to be careful. This surgery is not a permanent cure; it is possible that you'll have hemorrhoids again. Try to take a lot of fiber that will help you have easy bowel movement. Eat a lot of vegetables and always drink plenty of water. Good luck," he concluded.

By the time I left the University Teaching Hospital, the pain had decreased considerably. I had lost over ten pounds because of my liquid diet. I almost lost my balance because of being too light.

The first day I went to the office in preparation for resumption of teaching, I had a stack of letters awaiting me. Annie's handwriting stood out from the others in the heap. I quickly picked out that to read. I shook with excitement as I opened the letter. It was a long letter.

My dear Jo:

I know you must be very worried and at the same time wondering why you have not heard from me. I know that you will somehow feel that all has not been well with me and that is very true. Since I have been posted, you wouldn't have my current address. I have been very sick with malaria and typhoid that had been recurring when I thought I was already well. I thought I was going to die and thought every day of you, but couldn't write you. When you add the four or five days that I was sick before I was confined in a hospital bed for another three weeks, you can understand my long silence.

You know what happens in our hospitals. When I first went to the hospital and described my condition, without any tests I was given a full dose of Chloroquine tablets as if I had malaria. But as I remained weak and worse after taking the full dose of the prescribed medication, the doctor asked for blood tests on typhoid, which came out positive. By then I had lost appetite for any food, was wobbling on my feet, and looked pale. My friend Miriam was so good; she brought me food and visited every day. She stayed with me till just before nightfall when she left. A few other members of the youth corps also visited frequently.

I didn't want somebody else to let you know that I had been sick. I considered asking Miriam to write to you on my behalf, but that could cause you more serious concern to know that I was too sick in a hospital bed to even write you. Now that I am discharged, I write at the earliest possible time. I am about fully well now. The only thing is that I need time to get stronger, and that will come gradually. My appetite is improving, my energy coming back by the day.

I am currently doing my service at Government Teachers' College, GTC for short, Kano. I was able to change my posting to here from Bichi, which I felt would be too far if you wanted to visit me. Bichi is another two to three hours by taxi from Kano. I am teaching English language and literature here.

I am very eager to see you again. Even in the hospital bed, I thought every day of you. I still relish the aftertaste of our trip to Mubi and want the same again. I had never felt so good as in Mubi. Either it was a heaven on earth or a prelude to paradise. I will never forget the moments we shared together there. Once you arrive at GTC, Kano, ask of me or the two youth service ladies teaching English. I share a twobedroom apartment with Miriam outside but very close to the school compound.

How have you been since we were together last? I hope you are doing fine. You can visit anytime, preferably come on a Thursday or Friday so that we could have a weekend to ourselves. I teach only one *class on Friday very early in the morning and the rest of the day and the entire weekend are free.*

I look forward to your visit.
Very affectionately,
Annie

I cannot recollect how the rest of the week passed. I believe I taught on Tuesday and Wednesday as I made arrangements to travel to Kano on Thursday. Annie's letter had given me back the very strength that the surgery had taken away. I felt like a bull. I asked Samuel to accompany me. I was again bound for Kano.

I had made up my mind to stay at the University Guest House on Ibrahim Taiwo Road. When we arrived in Kano, I went to book for accommodation there before heading for Government Teachers' College at the other end of the city.

Annie had left the hospital the day that I was going in. She expected me the previous weekend and felt that since I couldn't make it that one, I must this one. My appearance was therefore expected. Annie was in the staff room. Seeing each other, we were oblivious of others and clasped ourselves warmly. We held to each other for minutes as Miriam waited to greet me. Miriam would have understood. The other teachers around must have looked on in wonderment. When we reluctantly broke from the embrace, Annie introduced me to her colleagues.

After the introduction and a few pleasantries, we went to the car to head for their apartment. Annie already knew Samuel and they exchanged greetings. I introduced Samuel, and she introduced Miriam.

"What happened to you? You have been sick too?" she asked, after we settled into the car.

"Sort of sick," I told her.

"No, you have been seriously sick as I can see," she said.

"I had an operation to remove piles that were troubling me," I explained.

"I understand it is a very painful procedure," she told me.

"Yes, nothing I had gone through before compares with the pain. In any case, it is all over now," I said.

She held my hand, squeezed my palm affectionately and looked into my eyes with the intensity of a healer checking on a patient.

"Thank God we are both now well," she intoned.

"Did you receive my letter?" she asked, after a brief pause.

"Of course, yes. It was after I left hospital."

"I am most happy you are here. Only God knows why both of us were hospitalized about the same time," she said.

Both of us might have had the same reason of not causing the other heartache in not letting the other know during the period of sickness.

Annie was a perfect hostess. She and Miriam entertained Samuel and me so warmly that I was overwhelmed. I was very well again. We ate very delicious food, *tuwo shinkafa* with vegetable soup, and drank tasteful wine.

"Both of you must be communicating through secret channels. Annie told me this morning that you'll come today. She was very sure," Miriam said.

"Why not?" Annie asked back rhetorically.

We looked at each other longingly. I seized the opportunity of Miriam's stepping into the bedroom to tell Annie that I had booked for an accommodation in town. She went in, I believe to tell Miriam that she would be leaving with me to town. She put a few dresses and toiletries in a bag and told me she was ready. We held each other's hands as we drove away.

We spent much of the night narrating our different experiences in hospital—how we felt, thoughts about the other, fear of death, and many more things. In my ward nobody died when I was there for the five days. It was a simple operation, they said, but no operation is free from the risk

95

of death. After all, there had been in these simple operations patients, who did not wake from the anesthesia. There could be cases of serious infection that brought complications to rather simple operations. Annie said five or more women in the female ward died while she was there. Some of the cases were already too bad before the patients came to the hospital. From our discussion, we were grateful to God for recovery. Life and death were so close, and sometimes a little delay or chance happening could lead to life or death. We also talked about other things. We always had something to talk about excitedly whenever together, but this time it was as if we had come back from the dead. We would no longer take good health for granted.

If Mubi was a prelude to paradise, my three days in Kano with Annie were days in paradise. She had asked Miriam to teach her Friday morning class and so we had all of Friday and Saturday to explore Kano, and we used the days to the fullest. After breakfast on Friday, we visited the Audu Bako Zoo and there spent three good hours watching animals behave like human beings. It was there that the theory of evolution came closest to reality for me. How could those apes not be the forerunners of humans in their behavior? The place was both a park and a zoo and the facility was well taken care of. There were also many visitors. As we saw the vast collection of wildlife, I wondered how much like animals we human beings were, and vice versa. After all, our folk tales teach that. Those animals, including the tortoise, hyena, and elephant, behave as we humans do. The elephant was very family-oriented, its young ones always by its side. So powerful and yet so patient, the elephant exercised power modestly. There were alligators, crocodiles, and others of their amphibian kind.

We were exhausted at the end of the tour and decided to go back to have lunch and rest before touring other parts of the city. At about three o'clock we set out for Bagauda Lake. The drive itself was most pleasurable. The fresh landscape reinforced our emotional excitement.

The open flat savannah brought back to me myths and tales of the Hausa people. Where was Zaki, the lion? I asked myself. It must be howling somewhere, hiding, or stalking some unfortunate animals beyond the pale of our eyes. Where was Kura, the hyena? It must be laughing in its belly at some unfortunate prey. Giwa, the elephant, must be strolling majestically with its offspring by its side. Are djinns ever visible? A limitless expanse of fields of corn, sorghum, millet, and groundnuts stretched before us. Who dare say that our peasants are not strong? They toiled on the soil available to them, and the yield was tremendous. The green leaves were like shields held against hunger. These people's industry gladdened us. The fifty-kilometer drive passed in a flash.

We toured the lake resort on foot. The lake had been man-made, but was full of water. It even had waves, no doubt stirred by strong winds common in the open savannah country. The hotel buildings had the architecture of Fulani homes. Round shelters with thatched roofs, almost conical, in shape. We did not intend to pass the night there, but were tempted to see the inside of the homes. The seemingly small size outside belied their roomy inside. They were very cool inside despite the scorching heat outside. People really know how to adapt to their own environment, however hostile it may be. We sat by the huge swimming pool watching swimmers and other tourists around. There were many white men and women in the pool. A few Africans, no doubt prosperous from their looks, also swam and played in the pool. After some thirty minutes, we left the swimming pool area.

Further away stood a baobab, a tree of immeasurable size in the fairly arid area. I wondered what underground currents fed it to that massive size in a parched landscape. Was the baobab the survivor of perennial desiccation that turned a once wet place into a semi-desert? It was a symbol of resilience, as it did not yield to drought and die off. Samuel, Annie, and I went to enjoy the mammoth tree's shade. We wondered from its size that it should be more than two hundred years old.

From Bagauda Lake, we drove to the nearby Rock Castle. It was already evening and the sky was darkening from increasing clouds, the breeze strengthening. Before Rock Castle was emblazoned a signpost, GIANT IN THE SUN. Rock Castle was really a giant hotel complex. Sculpted from a rocky expanse, the architecture displayed wonderful beauty. We went to the bar to have a cold drink after the exhausting tour. As we entered the car to begin our return to the city, flashes of lightning welcomed us. It was about seven-thirty in the evening and should naturally be a little dark. However, within minutes, it was pitch dark. The wind had picked up so much strength that we could feel the car rocking in its wake. We feared the wind might lift the car and throw us into the bush. It started to thunder too as the storm unleashed its power. I wanted us to stop by the roadside until the storm subsided. Samuel said stopping by the roadside was itself more dangerous than moving on because we stood a greater risk of being hit by other vehicles when stationary than if we continued. He drove at a very slow speed since it was almost nil visibility in spite of the bright headlamp. It was difficult to see the lights of oncoming vehicles too, and Samuel had to clamp down the brakes several times to avoid an accident.

And so, in the midst of lightning and thunder, sometimes appearing simultaneously, we crawled on. As we entered the city, a thunderous flash of lightning crashed as if beside our car. In a reflex reaction, Annie and I grabbed each other. We remained silent till we got to the Guest House. It was one of the longest-lasting storms, we learnt afterwards, in Kano. Thanks to Samuel's driving experience and extreme caution, we arrived home safely.

Despite the exhaustion, we talked almost all night again. We told each other more about our beginnings and we had detailed knowledge of the other's background and past. Annie told me she was the first of her mother's three children, two girls and a boy. Her sister was already married with two children. Her brother, her mother's youngest child, was in a secondary school in Keffi. In her father's polygamous compound, she was second to the first child of the first wife. Left to her father alone, he would have preferred her to marry early rather than go to secondary school. He was also at the beginning opposed to her going to the university.

"A woman's education," he had told her once, "is an unnecessary waste of money."

"But how can it be a waste of money if afterwards I get a good job and start sending you and Mama a good sum? Do you want me to just stay at home as a housewife and a cook and make babies?"

"What else will a woman do? If you marry a rich man, he should take good care of you," he told her.

"What if I married a poor man?"

"With your education already, you won't marry a poor man." "You see why education is important? If a little education already can make me not marry poor, then more education could make me not only rich but also perhaps marry rich."

That was long before her father and Nathan's father met and arranged their engagement. But once Annie was in the university, her father boasted of having the only female child studying English in a university in all of Nang. Upon graduation, he sang it out that his daughter was the first female graduate in Nang.

I told Annie about my parents and my hometown of Effurun, known for its powerful warriors in the olden days and still feared today by travelers. She wished my parents were still alive from the fond way in which I talked about them. She would tease me later with "Mother Hen," my pet name for my mother from the way she struggled with my father to lavish attention on me. Of my drunkard but amiable father, she had the equivalent in her paternal uncle, who rarely showed up in Nang. People tend to be two in the world, I told her.

I also told her about Maria, who was in Lagos with the children. She had told me about her "situation," as she put it.

"So we are both tied to some posts," I told Annie.

"Though not really married on my part," she replied.

By dawn we had come close to knowing all we needed to know about the other that we did not yet know. We were aware of the complications in our friendship but did not dwell on them. I would always fight alone the battle of loyalty in my head, but always be won over by feelings for Annie. I believe she went through the same struggle in her situation.

On Sunday morning we took Annie to her apartment and sat for about two hours to talk with Miriam. We could talk on and on for the rest of the day, but we had to leave to get back to Yerwa before dark. I drove on our way back, fully recovered from my surgery. I had sought and found my heart's content.

8

BENEDICTION BEFORE MASS

Let me go back to our last night in Kano. I took Annie back not only to my beginning but also to my life with Maria. I felt no inhibition telling her all as accurately as I knew. She had told me her own, the whole story of her traditional entanglement, and it was right I did the same.

Maria had been introduced to me after I broke with Ese, who wanted me to work in a corporation or company rather than teach. Ese had very harsh words for teachers, and I resented her for lack of understanding of other people's choices. People are different and they want different lifestyles. Choice is an inalienable right of every individual. What would make one happy might make another unhappy. Some choose wealth, others peace, and yet others fame. The only common denominator is choice.

"Teachers are failed ones that cannot get better jobs," she told me.

"So you mean I teach because I can't get any other type of job?" I asked.

"If you can, why do you waste your time talking and staining yourself with chalk?" she asked back.

"What do you expect from a good job?" I asked. "Success. Success. Success," she repeated. "What is success? How is it measured?" "Money. Money. Money," she replied. "What of fulfillment?" I further asked.

"How can an unsuccessful person ever describe himself or herself as fulfilled?" she countered.

I knew that, to her, success meant wealth. If she wanted to pursue wealth of money in a vulgar way, she should count me out of her life. Of course, for all the successes that would be in office jobs, I couldn't imagine myself in an administrative position in Shell or somewhere else that my age-mates were bribing and lobbying to get into. That would be a sedentary life that I was not ready for. I wanted to be relatively free in whatever work I chose to do. And teaching appealed to me. Teaching afforded me all the many holidays to do what I wanted. Teaching would make me search for knowledge even as I taught others. Teaching, not as a trained teacher with a bachelor's degree in education and carrying about charts. Ese wouldn't marry a teacher by whatever name, graduate, postgraduate, or whatever. I was disappointed, but felt I would some day meet somebody who would love a teacher or me.

I got to know Maria through a friend of mine. He knew that I broke with Ese because I wanted a serious relationship—I wanted to settle down, as we used to say. A time came for a man when he wanted to marry and be stable, I thought. I came across many young women, some in school and others already out of the university. In hindsight, I did not know what type of woman I was looking for as my wife. I wanted somebody educated and presentable, but that was a very wide net that would catch too many young women in Warri. After Ese, I was very wary of women who wanted high life—expensive clothes, high fashion, fine cars, and others. With many the discussions did not go beyond the ordinary, material things that only money could buy. I withdrew from such people because I knew we had different values. I was like a rabbit that had escaped from a trap, I kept away from any bent stick on the ground—it might be another trap and I might not be twice lucky!

Neither Maria nor I threw one at the other. She was introduced as the sister of a friend's wife. We drifted towards each other gradually, slowly but intentionally. It was as if both of us felt it was time to have a partner, marry, and settle down. We passed each other at the Continuing Education Center for months without noticing each other until our being introduced. I taught Literature on a part-time basis, she studied Commercial subjects full-time. So we really did not meet at the CEC, unless we had an appointment.

After several months of being friends, a period in which we must have been studying each other without saying so, we went to watch a film together at Delta Cinema. It was the most central of the three film houses then in Warri, just behind the Magistrate Court in the mainly commercial district of town. We asked the taxi driver to drop us beside Barclays Bank, opposite the court, on Warri-Sapele Road and walked the short distance to the cinema house. The road to the cinema house was thronged with young people, a sign that a popular film was to be shown that night. Though there were no newspapers with film reviews in Warri, yet within days of a popular film in town the youths knew about it. This night it was an Indian film, "Love in Bombay."

It was a very noisy scene. The audio system was poor and harsh— you had to strain your ears to hear anything. To compound this was the noise of the film watchers, especially from the general seating area. The second-class and first-class watchers appeared more restrained in their responses to the happenings in the story. Of course, those people were more matured. Young rascals filled the general area. Indian films were very popular, more so a love one like "Love in Bombay." Despite the loud whistling and moaning, Maria and I followed the story. Two young people in love, but their parents would not agree for them to marry. They tried to escape to a place where they were not known, but the woman was caught. She later set herself ablaze, preferring to die rather than live without her boyfriend. She was badly burnt but did not die. After the man learnt of her attempted suicide, he went to her. He could barely recognize his love. After she called his name, he embraced the disfigured woman. The parents then let them do what they had wanted to do all along—marry. Before the ceremony took place, the woman suddenly died. It was a tragic love story. Many spectators hissed their disappointment as the woman died.

Leaving the cinema house, we went to my apartment. We prepared *jollof* rice with fried fish. By the time we had eaten, it was already very late. We realized that it would not be wise for Maria to go home that night. Fortunately, she was spending the weekend with her elder sister, who knew we were friends. It was fortunate because there was no way her parents would go to bed without assuring themselves that she was back, if she had gone out with any man. I had already heard stories of how protective her mother was. She kept her daughters in line with an iron hand, and whoever among them took the wrong course would feel sorry for it. Her elder sister had suffered beatings for talking innocently with men or coming late from playing with her mates. Now married, she indirectly sanctioned our friendship and, we believed, expected us to marry some day.

Much as both of us felt uncomfortable about it, she had to pass the night in my place. We felt that her sister would understand and not report to her parents. After all, we had looked for an opportunity like this for months to get to know each other much better. We talked as we had not talked before.

Maria asked me about my parents and I told her about them. My father had four wives, who helped him in his palm oil-producing business. "How is he able to take care of four women?" she asked. "I don't know, but he seems to handle the responsibility well," I told her.

She muttered "Huun!" which I could not interpret. She was no doubt surprised about my polygamous background compared to her monogamous Christian parents. She did not see herself as a perfect Christian, but she had restrained herself a bit, thanks to her Roman Catholic faith.

Not that we were not afraid before going to bed, but the consequence came as we had feared and expected—Maria became pregnant, a scandal for her Roman Catholic parents. It did not take her experienced mother too long to notice that the vomiting, weakness, and the cool shine on her daughter's face were early signs of pregnancy. Her parents did not ask her for whom she was pregnant. They knew the culprit, since their older daughter must have told them of my interest in Maria. Their daughter was already a marriageable woman anyway, and they waited for me to take the next step.

How word reached the reverend father who knew her family very well, only God could tell.

"What example are you showing my parishioners?" Father Brown queried Maria's parents.

There were many do-gooders in the church and word always got to the reverend father in no time whenever a parishioner deviated from the church canon, and it was known. Father Brown thus had enough eyes and ears prying into the lives of his flock. Confession though was confidential, and he did not act on what he heard from his familiar parishioners. Still, this made his church people to hide as much as they could of their own moral indiscretions from the church authorities and their fellow Christians. Rather, they confessed specific sins in general terms, or sometimes invented sins they had not committed to seem fallible but not too bad Christians.

Father Brown had summoned Maria's parents as soon as he got wind of the immoral act of their daughter. He understood well that Maria would not agree to come with her parents to see him; hence he did not bother to include her in his summons that he called an invitation. He knew the grip he had over older people, who deferred to him as to their lord.

"We are ashamed of her action," Pa Numa explained apologetically.

"Shut up!" Father Brown shouted, as if reprimanding his child.

Father Brown was in his mid-thirties. He had joined the priesthood relatively young. After only three years as an assistant priest in Cork, he had requested to be posted to Africa. He got his wish and was sent to the Delta Diocese of Nigeria, where after another three years he became the main officiating priest; he was next to the bishop in rank.

"You have disgraced our church," he went on. "Fornication is a grievous sin. Both of you couldn't stop your daughter from sinning!"

"We have always shown her good examples at home. And Maria till now has always been good," Mrs. Numa said.

"No, her action is indefensible and unacceptable. Both of you are negligent of parental duty and are as guilty as your daughter. I suspend both of you from receiving the Holy Communion from today on. Live with the sins of your daughter whom you couldn't bring up as a good Catholic girl," Father Brown pronounced with finality.

Father Brown, like most white people, never responded positively to begging. And so, instinctively, Maria's parents only answered, "Yes, Father." Simultaneously, they made the sign of the cross and retreated from the reverend's holy presence. They had stood all along before the seated priest.

Maria was twenty-five years old. It didn't matter that she was no longer a minor. The trouble was her pregnancy, a visible exhibit of her corruption. She had confessed to the same reverend father several times about temptations before her pregnancy became visible, and the priest always forgave her and asked her to resist the temptations of the flesh. He had told her to say "Hail Mary" a hundred times and was getting short of punishments before this occurrence. Maria left her parents' home to live with me.

Maria delivered a baby boy. My mother was very happy. She had been nudging me on to marry and from the day I told her of my friend's pregnancy, she was overjoyed. I brought Maria home for introduction, and my mother was most pleased.

"Now, I'll have a grandchild!" she shouted.

She knelt by the right-hand side of the threshold and called several names, most likely of her ancestors, and gave thanks. I was so moved that I knelt beside her. And when Maria saw us down, she also came down on her knees. I was surprised because she always railed against ancestor worship, in keeping with her Roman Catholic beliefs. I had failed in the short period of our relationship to impress on her that Christianity should not be against African culture and customs. Though of non-Christian parents, I had gone to Catholic schools, served at Mass for many years, and knew so much about the church. I scored an "A" in religious knowledge in the school certificate examinations. But these did not stop me from respecting my parents and their ancestors.

Maria and I had set out to observe the other and watch how things went before talking about marriage. Circumstances had changed things. There are courses charted already and we just have to follow them. We settled for a traditional marriage. There was to be neither court marriage nor church marriage for us. She called the marriage "Benediction before Mass," since it was taking place after her delivery. But it was as good as any other, I felt. She did not say it to me, but she knew that we scandalized her parents in living together before any form of marriage.

Her parents were lukewarm towards our idea of a traditional marriage, but they had to be polite hosts to my family representatives during the bride-price paying ceremony. So when we went to their place in Warri, the customary light-hearted banter prevailed. Kola nuts, gin, and a token payment, as tradition demanded, were presented. There was singing and dancing, and everyone had a good time. I was happy at how well the ceremony went. And I was so pleased that even Christian parents, contrary to my earlier belief, did not forget their own customs, for all they said against them when in the church or before reverend fathers.

Soon after the bride-price paying ceremony, Maria told me that Father Brown sent for her parents. He should have received a report of the activities from one of his telltale flock more than eager to be in good standing with him. Father Brown offered to rescind the suspension of Maria's parents from receiving the Holy Communion if she and I came to marry in the church. I was not prepared for that. The priest was not going to use intimidation of Maria's parents to bring us to his altar. He was being clever in telling the parents to tell Maria, so as to make her feel guilty and pressurize me for both of us to succumb to his desire. What he had not got earlier, he now wanted by other means!

For me, marriage once sanctified traditionally was enough. Was marriage strengthened by how many times over rituals were performed? I did not want to re-marry the person I had already married. Our family elders had blessed the relationship and that would do for me. The voice of the people, I had learnt at school, is the voice of God.

One Sunday afternoon I received or rather played host to unexpected guests. Father Brown and Maria's mother came to our twobedroom apartment. It was about late in the afternoon, about four o'clock. For all my surprise, it appeared Maria knew about the visit beforehand.

She had persisted for weeks about the necessity of having our baby son baptized. When I said that the child should choose his religion when eighteen or old enough to know what his choice meant, she asked me why I did not wait for so long before my own baptism.

"But I was baptized under duress," I told her.

"Did somebody snatch you from your parents' home to the church to dip into water?" she asked.

"No. But without acceding to baptism, I should have been asked to withdraw from the Catholic elementary school, the only school in that area. There are many schools around nowadays and that leverage is gone," I tried to explain. "Let our child be baptized," she pleaded.

"The priest will have to come to our home to do it; if not, I won't go to him and give him the opportunity to entrap us," I said as a compromise.

"Who knows? He may one day find his way to our home and baptize Omose," she told me.

I had already committed myself to her. Maria might have gone behind me to her mother who must have gone to the priest who believed baptizing my son would be the first step of bringing Maria and, by extension, me back to his church. For this first step of bringing a recalcitrant man back to his church, Father Brown was ready to take the extraordinary step of coming to my own apartment to baptize my son.

The rest of the visit was very uneventful. I insisted that my son's name be Omose that my mother gave to him and not Patrick that the priest suggested. How clever, I thought, the reverend father was to promote the name of his country's patron saint at the expense of African names! He bowed to my insistence, but I knew he was merely stooping to conquer me someday to come. The priest set about the rite very officiously and left as soon as he completed it. Maria and her mother were very pleased that Omose was now a Christian and not a pagan, condemned to hell should he die. I internally lauded the priest for his tenacity in pursuing every strategy available in his attempt to bring Maria and me to the altar to be further blessed as husband and wife, which we already were.

Within a relatively short time, we had one more child, a girl we named Titi. Maria took her to the church to get baptized—I did not accompany her. To my surprise, Father Brown asked of me, her husband. He seemed to have accepted the inevitable. We soon left Warri for Lagos. I had got a teaching assistantship from the University of Lagos and was planning to go for doctoral studies overseas. I felt relieved that I was outside the pressures of Father Brown.

9

LETTERS

Time passed fast. It had been twelve years since we met last, twelve years since Annie married. I had since returned from Yerwa to Lagos, where I had been Head of Department for two terms of three years each. I had just been promoted to the position of a professor.

Annie and I kept in touch by writing, which both of us were adept at. Once in a while, there was a prolonged period of silence, which somehow soon got broken by one or the other. We were almost like pen pals and knew we had to keep on writing to assuage the other's torment from absence. We wrote about anything possible, about ourselves, national politics, and, above all, about poetry. We frequently sent poems to each other. With the constant writing, it appeared as if we saw or met each other all the time.

Any time I received a letter from Annie, I was usually upbeat. The handwriting was clear, a firm blue artwork. I experienced a heart's throb, then a vision of her emblazoned in the air like a vast flag of a nation of patriots unfurled from one horizon to another. Nothing mattered than opening the letter and enjoying its content.

Another of her letters had come. The handwriting was unmistakably hers. I suspected this letter must be the reply to my letter to her that was brief, strong and ending with "What do we do now?"

I had to ask that after Dr. Nathan Goomsay wrote me a very curious letter. Strange that he wrote me at all, but stranger still the content of his letter. How he got my address, I could not guess. But Annie would tell me later how he rifled through her cupboard, bags, and everything in her room to get a lead into the direction of her heart's feelings.

Here's what he wrote, a typed letter that I suspected but was not too sure he might have either copied Annie or kept the copy for himself. Or my copy might just be the only one. All the same, I felt Annie should read this letter and know the state of things.

Dear Dr. Ogbe,

I would be grateful if you would stop further communication with my wife, Mrs. (Dr.) Anna Goomsay, a former student of yours at the University of Yerwa.

Your use of God's given gift of poetry to seduce my wife should please stop. Write your poems and publish for its academic value only and stop sending her copies with dedications in it. All she does at home is read your poems or write in response to them. Both of you should not take me to be a fool. I know what is going on between you two. It cannot be a good thing but an unholy relationship which both of you should stop immediately. I have read some of the poems both of you have written and what is in them is unacceptable to me. Both of you should be ashamed of your behavior. She is married and I believe you are also married. Do you people ever think of that? Do you know that the parties involved in marriage should hold the institution in high esteem? Both of you are educated and should know that by now.

Please do not make any attempt to see her whenever you are in this vicinity again as you did last time around. Anna was bold enough to write the details of your meeting in her diary and she feels she can hide things from me. She is making a mistake; I have my eyes and ears and know what is happening. Teachers should be trusted—taking advantage of the weaker sex is sinful. Start by asking your publishers to remove the dedication, "For Annie again."
Yours
Dr. Nathan Goomsay, MB, BS

I didn't think he expected a reply from me, and so I didn't write back. Replying, of course, would have enraged him the more and led us to exchange insults. Somewhere along the line, if we exchanged letters, he would have dragged Annie into it or used my letters as exhibit to confirm his wife's straying, as he saw it. The more distant and mysterious I was from them, the better for my relationship with Annie. I was not going to answer his accusation of seducing his wife with poetry. I felt flattered and happy that he didn't say that I seduced his wife with money or something else that would demean our relationship. Everywhere around, men seduced women with money or other material things. But ours would be a unique form of seduction.

I believe Annie must have told him several times that I didn't teach her any course in her final semester when I arrived in Yerwa, but he wouldn't believe that we met outside of class. He had to give our friendship a bad name to cast aspersions on our integrity.

I really visited and saw Annie for the first time since here marriage thirteen years ago. I had gone to the University of Bukuru to "moderate examination papers" in the English Department. We were able to link up and she drove from Barkin Ladi to visit me where I stayed in Bukuru, some thirty-five kilometers away. We chatted and read poems to each other, but we did not have a physical relationship. Sex did not come to our minds and we did not want to complicate more the other's life. We knew from the last meeting before her marriage that our relationship would not continue to be physical.

Annie's courier letter came by United Parcels Services, hence the same white and red large plastic envelope as Dr. Nathan Goomsay had used. The letter announced her severance from the "patriarch, who torments me emotionally, physically, and psychologically and has been so insensitive."

She continued. *I have reached a point in my unpleasant marriage life that I have decided once and for all to strip and purge myself of any material and emotional attachment to this unpleasant experience that is marriage.*

I do not want to leave the marriage for the sake of my children—he will certainly try to keep them from me, and I want to be part of their upbringing. The children have seen for themselves how he mistreats me, and I won't like him to have the chance to poison their minds against me. He is capable of vicious poison. But while I will stay in the house for the sake of my dear little ones, at the same time I am wresting out of any further encumbrances occasioned by over-dependence in emotional terms on a husband of my type who does not care a bit about my feelings! I am giving you the facts of my situation as they have always been so that you know the hell that I am experiencing. You are my true witness. With the position I have now taken (so that I do not lose my mind), I believe the battle is half won!

I really have had enough of humiliation and suffering in the name of staying married. Now, while I remain married, it is only in name as I have my wits about me. I will never give in to self-pity and waste away. I have resolved to remain strong and steadfast in my work and I have the confidence that with your love and kind assistance, these sad experiences I have had all through my life will be history.

It has dawned on me that my husband is neither keen nor interested in my success. My modest accomplishments career-wise had troubled him and made him so unsure of himself. Why should a published collection of poems bring so much rancor? And why quarrel with my involvement with the state branch of NOW? My colleagues and I are only trying to assist our people in sending their girls to school rather than keep them at home to wait for marriage. Our secondary school girls, especially those in the drama groups, all look up to going to institutions of higher learning such as this polytechnic or the university. The female student population here has increased tremendously. I don't want to be praised for it, but our women's groups have played a big role in this turn-around. I need no problems at home so that I can work harder.

Our macho men prefer women who they can bark at, trample upon, and throw away like some menstrual rags after use! Unfortunately, my man knows that I am not that kind, nor do I even deserve in the least to be so treated. I have always respected him, cooked, and raised his children for him even when he was mean to me. You see, the more I reflect on the years I have spent all alone, keeping myself and the kids, my husband and his damned attitude aggravate my grief the more. He is a chronic ingrate who not one day will tell you one good thing for the sacrifices that you made on his behalf. That is part of the sadism in him, his not acknowledging a good turn done to him. How he feels that I should repeat a good turn when the past ones are not acknowledged reflects his shallow or miscalculating mind.

Needless to say now, I have absolved myself from any oath of marriage to him. I know how you will feel disappointed in this, more so as you have consistently written that I try to make the best of the marriage. However, I have to severe myself from him to go on with my life. I cannot remain his with his type of behavior. Understand my plight and accept my reasons and feelings.

This letter raised mixed feelings in me. I felt sad about what my friend was going through. At the same time, I was delighted in a strange way at the turn of events. Sooner or later, we would have to decide what to do with our relationship. Was this letter not direct enough? For how long would you allow your true friend and love to be abused before intervening? Since she was married, had I any right to intervene in her problem with her man? Was I a married man myself not going too far to even listen to the complaints of a woman married to another man no matter the circumstances? I tried to answer these questions as frankly as I could and came to the conclusion that I had the responsibility not only as her witness and friend, but as a human being to stop any torture and abuse of a

114

fellow human being. Are these not what writers and others carry placards about often to draw attention to marital abuse and domestic violence? Have I not heard many victims of spousal abuse giving chilling testimonies of their mistreatments? Have many women not suffered to the end, in the absence of anyone to help them? Have many not been killed or died as a result of the abuse? Is this not a crime against humanity on a domestic scale? Must I wait or delay until he did her more hurt? There were many questions to ask about Annie's condition. Each contemplated answer asked for responsibility of helping those in such dire need.

Tears welled up in my eyes. I felt personally hurt by Annie's hurt. I felt an emotional anguish and could only conjecture the degree of physical, psychological and emotional abuse she bore in the name of marriage. It was a matter of time and I would take on Nathan headlong, if the abuse continued. The duel he had been spoiling for was already in the making, and I prayed that Annie be not crushed in the middle and should triumph at the end. I had earlier pledged to her "Should it come to the stage for you to leave, know that I am here for you."

She disposed of my torments, those hammer blows which had tortured me every minute for years. She acquitted me in the trial in which the prosecution accused me of adultery, of putting into peril another person's marriage. The prosecution pointed fingers at me for violating somebody else's sacred space. He tried to convince the jury of sanctimonious lords that I was a thief who should be punished severely. And my defense countered about using laws of one game to judge another. Could love be enforced, if not there? Should one allow his love to be brutalized, just because the abuser claims right to the abused? Are adults not free to live their lives the way they so choose? By not meeting her and also not having any physical relationship with her since her marriage, was our love not pure enough to be absolved from any insults?

Yes, I had asked myself who was right or who was wrong in this matter. Were we all right or all wrong, this tripartite muddle? All of us could be wrong and at the same time right. But how could any of us, especially Annie and I, be more rational than our hearts dictated to us? As the Sierra Leonean poet, Syl Cheney-Coker, asks in a poem, who will call the volcano to order in its boiling or fire-spitting rage?

If he does not care for me, why is he jealous of who cares for me? He does not like me. Why is he bothered that somebody else so much loves me and he harasses him with a threatening letter? He torments me and yet feels hurt that somebody has the capacity to heal the wounds he inflicts on me.

This letter was a direct response to the copy of Nathan's letter to me, which I had sent to her. Her letter carried the assurances that I needed. She continued.

Don't mind him. Don't engage in a debate with him. He is a madman, and if you take on a madman in a quarrel or fight, you'll lose your dignity. He has no shame, nothing to lose. Leave him.

I apologize for his insults. A sensible person would have talked to me rather than write to you, a stranger. I am sorry that he has to insult you because of me.

She then talked about her health in spite of everything, the two kids gone to secondary school, and her backdated promotion to senior lecturer. And she ended with "Always yours, Annie." I had to buy and send her a congratulatory card, a blank card with a red rose opening out. I wrote my congratulatory message on the card. She was moving forward in her profession in spite of many obstacles, especially at home, and that was a very great achievement.

Part III: Annie

10

THE MISCARRIAGE

Dear Jo:

It must have been long after he discovered from my poems and yours that you had been around as an external examiner at the University of Bukuru and stayed a few days longer because of me. He got right the hint from your poems—you wrote the date and place of most of the poems at the end of each. Mine were also dated. If you searched dark places, you would likely chance into some dirt or unpleasant things. He secretly entered my room to read the poems. How he knew that you were not in Yerwa, as he had up till then believed, but in Lagos I don't know. He would have fared very well in the Secret Service if he chose spying as a career.

To him, you were always around anyway and I secretly went out to meet you whenever I wished under his nose. Of course, you had long gone back, but his jealousy and sense of insecurity provided a mindset of your continuous presence wherever I happened to be. After all, he asked me why I wanted to go alone to the village to see my parents and yet would not accompany me when I asked him to. They had moved back to the village, since they did not like living in Bukuru. My father did not like the city and wanted to go back to his other wives who remained at home. He also wanted to continue with his farming, which, though brought him little, gave him something fulfilling in his life. I remember seeing him planting fresh cactuses to demarcate his farm and looking with immense satisfaction at the corn and millet growing up. His eyes glowed with a bright light that life in the town could not spark. He also demarcated his wives' gardens, which were near our compound and where they grew vegetables. A distance away from home was his farm for yams and millet. He enjoyed leaving home during the farming season and he must have missed that in town.

I learnt that my mother was sick and I wanted to give her all the support I could muster. She was living alone, since all of us, her children, were grown up and gone our separate ways. Living in a polygamous compound of many children and adults, she had frequently confided in me about her loneliness. Every household stuck together and she was alone in hers now. I went on Saturday and returned on Sunday. She had had pneumonia, and had almost recovered. She wondered how I had heard of her illness, but she was very pleased that I came to see her. You know a mother will always appreciate her child's concern. Still in her late fifties, she was not yet old. Hard work in the village though was taking its toll on her.

When I came back, my lord husband did not ask me about the condition of my mother whom I had told him I was going to visit. I still had to tell him that she had pneumonia and was recovering well. But he had his insidious ways of searching my handbags for anything. Was he expecting my lover to be at my parents' home? Was he so guilty of his attitude towards me that, as our tradition used to allow spouse-abused women to do, I had taken a lover that my parents sanctioned? Nobody talked of that old practice nowadays because women abused in marriage often chose either to leave their marital homes for elsewhere or to deal with the problem their individual ways.

I expected his secret search and threw my handbag with tampons on the chair to excite his curiosity. The bait worked. After opening and seeing it, he flung it down as if it was not a neat thing. He must be crazy or mindless to expect me to go and see another man at my parents'.

We rarely turned to each other in bed and I did not have any feeling for him. But somehow, it still happened. Quality of sex has nothing to do with a chance happening. Conception has nothing to do with the passion of those making love. Many women conceive from rape. He had on many occasions virtually forced himself into me (I would have said raped me, if the Nigerian Constitution did not say that a husband could not rape his wife!), because he did not encourage or prepare me but just climbed and forced his way through and withdrew as soon as he was done in a half minute. You would pity him for whatever joy he felt he derived from what, if we shared it together, would be a joyful feast. He did things with so much haste, as if holding on to the next minute would rob him of something he was afraid to lose.

When the days for my normal menstruation were passing, I was thinking of irregularity creeping into my monthly cycle. At thirty-seven, I was no longer young. With age, the body changes into a slower rhythm. For us women, such surprising games of nature are frequent, from what I hear older women say. I thought my turn had come to experience the ambushes of nature in my body. Though not clockwork precise, two to four days later had been the maximum for me all the years. I always had signs, which had now become routine pain in the abdomen and a slight headache. I waited for the signs as I was on the lookout for any stains. I had on my tampon in anticipation of the monthly visitor. Nothing came the usual way.

So, after a week passed, I knew I was again stuck with his seeds. You remember that I told you that I wanted a girl. Under normal circumstances, having a girl with two boys would be ideal. But it had been a point of contention in my heart and mind. Much as I wanted a girl for a child, was I ready to bear another child for a man who did not care for me? Was conception not supposed to be a sign of love? How would you take it, when you heard? Won't you accuse me of separating means from ends, form from content? In an ideal world where things go right, yes; everything has to be a perfect blend of means and ends, form and content. But my world, from the initial mistake of going on with the pledge in a drunken gathering of two families, has never been a perfect one. So, don't think that I didn't think of you—I certainly did, always did as I still do.

I was sure I had conceived before telling my husband. I had learnt to do things at my convenience before him. My seeming confidence rattled him—it was one of the things, I believe, he tried to understand about me. Where did this confidence come from? Where would this confidence lead her? He must have asked himself many questions about me.

As he turned towards me in bed, in one of his many restless turns at night, I knew he was still awake. It was then that I told him that I was pregnant—I had not menstruated at its normal time and there were signals flashing in my body of the beginning of a new experience. After all, I was no longer a novice in this, after going through it twice.

"What?" he thundered.

120

I shrank back in shock. I expected a kiss, some tender response in the form of a warm embrace, jovial banter, or reciprocal congratulations. But it was part of his habit not to give me what he felt I needed or what he felt would give me the least pleasure or fulfillment.

"I am pregnant," I re-stated.

He suddenly got up, as if stung by an insect, and left the bed towards the sitting room. I knew he was preparing to hurt me and so I readied myself not to give him the pleasure of seeing me either cry out or follow him to be pushed aside. I knew what he wanted. He must have gone to the refrigerator for a bottle of Guinness because I heard it open and close. There was clacking of glasses as he took one from the cupboard. Then I heard him trip over something in the dark and shout: "Damn it!" There had been one of the usual blackouts in town as soon as we went to bed. I wondered what he was celebrating without me, the conceived one? Can there be happiness without sharing? I could not tell what he had in mind. His heart was closed to me.

After about a half-hour, he breezed back to the bed like a hurricane. He had fueled himself for his sadistic taunts and he would keep me sleepless with suppressed tears.

"You are not pregnant. If you are, it's not from me; it is not from me. You know whom you met secretly," he pronounced with a ridiculing voice. "What do you mean?" I asked.

"You know what I mean. One of your lovers, from around or far away," he answered.

Within me I wished it had been really you. I would have danced and danced over it. What could be more pleasing to me than having a baby with you? Nothing would please me more. But it was his, unfortunate as it was.

"Why couldn't it be you that impregnated me?" I asked.

Sometimes an opponent could reduce you to his or her mean level. I wanted to embarrass him as he was doing to me.

121

"I am not the one," he said emphatically.

He avoided my question. But I would not argue with my husband about the paternity of this child. I *knew* it was his.

"Since I married you, I have not slept with another person, whatever happened before then," I told him.

"What do you do with your secret lovers when you meet them? Laugh and leave each other? Don't take me to be a fool," he responded.

"I have no lover or lovers. I may have friends who happen to be men but not in the sense you are thinking of," I told him.

"You have found a fool," he said as he laughed coarsely. My man's voice was loud and I knew the two boys must have awakened and would be straining to hear what was amiss again. I prayed that this would not develop into another beating that would make the children to cry as I cried. No good parent would want to cause anguish for the children.

For weeks on weeks, my husband intensified nagging me. I was not pregnant for him but for Dr. Ogbe or somebody else around, he sang into my ears. Again, I pitied him. We never had time even when both of us were at home to deliberate on anything. Oil and water, our people say, don't mix.

Here was a medical doctor who was not using his skills. His education had been futile. I wondered if he still remembered there was blood or paternity test to confirm the father of a disputed baby. But my Dr. Goomsay had never been a rational man in spite of his medical training.

I did not care about his denial of responsibility for my conception. The plant should bear an undeniable fruit. It was only that I wouldn't like my child, or anybody else's child for that matter, to grow up and be like this man. At least, not like him in character. I wanted a daughter, and may it be so; I prayed.

For the next several months almost every word from his mouth to me was barbed. If I did not resist, he would drive each one like a nail into my heart. I believe he was more than capable of murder from the manner he treated me.

I was away from home for a four-day conference in Ilorin. He must have seen the invitation letter I left on the dining table before I informed him of my plans to participate in the conference. I was reacting to his spying tactics by leaving in places what I wanted him to see. He must be feeling that he was very smart. It is good for a fool to think he is wise sometimes. He was not interested in whatever would advance me professionally. He wanted me not to have self-pride in my work so that he could exercise his patriarchal vanity over me. He didn't care if I was not promoted; in fact, he might be happy that I stood still in my work as he expected me to be in the house.

"Who will give me food?" he asked in a cold tone mixed with harshness.

"Celia will put your food on the table. I will prepare enough food to last the duration of my absence," I explained.

"Is Celia my wife?" he asked.

I felt I did not need to answer his question. I was not his slave and I had my own free will and freedom.

I left for Ilorin. He did not stop me, but he did not ask how I got money to go or how I was going. He must have thought that with all my money spent in the upkeep of the house, I would not have enough money for traveling and accommodation. I ignored his sulking face. My department head had written the Rector after I informed him of my intention to participate in the conference. I was fortunate to have five thousand naira approved for me to spend. I always counted on the Polytechnic's support for my academic development.

The conference was a success. It gave me an opportunity to mix with colleagues. I learnt a lot from the more experienced participants. The keynote address by Professor Baro Tite was most inspiring. He gave an hour-long lecture without a scrap of paper to look at. It takes so much knowledge, so much experience, and so much self-confidence to do that. Basically, he says literature may be fiction but, in fact, it is an accurate reflection of life and society. What could be more accurate? And it was the style of presentation that clarified and brought fresh insight into what could be seen as a commonplace subject. At the end, everyone stood up and gave the learned professor an ovation. I wanted to work hard and get to be a chief lecturer or professor someday. My paper on "Empowering Women for National Development" was well received and I felt great. Many respondents agreed that a nation in which women were not educated and not valued could not be great because it would be utilizing half its human resources like an industry working at half capacity.

The four days away brought me respite from the civil war at home. The air at Ilorin was fresher than I was used to breathing. I had a nice room in Kwara Hotel, up on the seventh floor, from where I could look out and see much of the sprawling town. There was so much of luxury in the room and I let myself go to relish it. I did not have to prepare food for anybody, I occasionally asked for my meals to be brought to my room. I did not have to do chores I was used to at home. Above all, nobody barked at me. I cherished the silence while alone in the room. I felt a heavy load had been removed from my head. My occasional headaches disappeared.

I saw myself as being in temporary exile, which was gaining ground in the country. Many critics of the dictatorial government escaped to other countries to avoid arrest, harassment, or even being assassinated. Those who confronted tyranny frontally had either languished in jail or been killed. The casualties were many. Away I breathed freedom. But I was bound to return, much as I relished my freedom and sanity outside, to the domestic dictator. I was returning to my work and to my children.

Barkin Ladi was not too far from Ilorin, when you think of it, as far as road travel was concerned; about seven hours apart. However, the roads were bad with potholes and peeled tar cover. These were roads done by "emergency" contractors, who collected millions of naira for shoddy unprofessional work. Roads that were on paper resurfaced only a year ago were no roads at all. Because of the bad state of the roads, drivers meandered and stopped suddenly here and there for almost the entire journey. The driver always tried to hold the brakes but could not avoid running into some of the deep potholes. The shock absorbers of the car were bad and nothing soft cushioned the seats. Dust from passing cars and trucks flew into our car and we were covered with brown. I arrived back home feeling very exhausted. It was normal for me at this stage to be weak, but the travel exacerbated my fatigue.

As I expected, a sour face welcomed me home. I was used to his ugly side. That night once he knew I was gone to bed, he came too. He turned away as usual and after a while, as if he had left something undone before coming to bed, got up. He went to the side of the wardrobe where he kept his briefcase and brought it to the bed. He opened it and brought out my poems. Why he had to lock up my poems in his bag, as if they would fly or disappear from the house, I did not know. He flaunted the sheets of paper at me. He must have read them carefully and appeared very prepared to confront me about my feelings and ideas.

"You have been writing a lot lately," he said.

That would be taken as a compliment, if it came from a different type of man who had been used to encouraging his wife and one who had shown interest in poetry as an art form. But Nathan was not that kind of man who liked artistic expressions. No compliments about my poetry from the man who not only held my room's keys without my permission but secretly opened the room, and searched handbags, books, and poems. I did not answer him.

"Look at this," he said, throwing me a poem.

"What type of mother would have an affair and record it for her children and the whole world to know about?"

I maintained my silence. There was no need telling him that there was no affair as such in the sense he thought of it; there was no sexual relationship. A poem cannot be hard fact, since though rooted in reality it is often imagined. It seemed my silence closed his mouth from thrusting his barbed words at me.

He had carefully selected what he wanted to confront me with. He did not ask about the poems in which I raged against injustice, against patriarchy, or those in praise of motherhood. It was my veiled love poems that he saw fit to flaunt at me. I still believe he did not understand those poems, but he guessed they were love poems because they were dedicated to JO, which by now in his surveillance he should have discovered as Jo Ogbe.

"And what is the communion you shared other than sex?" he asked.

I did not utter a reply. His mind was too shallow to understand that there were other means of communion beside sex. The best way to stop somebody talking harshly to you is to respond with silence. I had discovered a fresh weapon with which to confront him and also defend myself.

Within days of returning from Ilorin, malaria knocked me down. The first day I attributed my fatigue to mere exhaustion. But my mouth developed a bitter taste and several rashes flared on my upper lip. When I started to feel cold and hot at the same time, I knew that I had fever. Since my doctor husband did not care about my condition, I went to a nearby clinic for treatment, which usually consisted of a full dose of Chloroquine tablets or a series of injection. I knew I had to eat before the injection, which should not be given to one with an empty stomach. That was proclaimed in every clinic so that doctors and nurses would not be held responsible for any patient's problem. Despite the food I took, I was still dazed after the injection and almost passed out. I regained my full consciousness and managed to walk the short distance home.

From that night, I started bleeding. I helplessly witnessed the fetus bleed away. I miscarried. What a waste!

126

My husband knew I was sick, but did not ask what was wrong with me. I gave him his food when it was time for it. He left his clothes for me to wash, but I asked Celia to wash them. He had the habit of throwing down his clothes after wearing them just once and he expected them to be washed and ironed by me. For some months I had refused to iron the clothes and he used to pay "Daddy," whose real name was Peter, from the neighboring compound to iron them for him. I was despondent from the loss. Four months of carrying what could have been my third child, perhaps the daughter I wanted. All was for naught. I lost the pregnancy, drop by drop.

He soon knew that I had miscarried. Who knows whether he felt that I was mischievously pulling his leg with my announcement of a pregnancy? He was, however, not the sort to cast jokes with. He had nothing doing at home, so he riveted his eyes on whatever I did.

"I thought you were pregnant?" he asked.

He deserved no response. He must have observed from my using a sanitary pad or seen bloodstains in the underwear I tossed aside that the embryonic baby's sack had deflated. "What have you done to my baby?" he asked, to my total dismay.

I was sad and confused. Did he like my pregnancy? If he did, he had not shown it to me all the months I had told him I had conceived.

"I hope your lovers have not asked you to abort the pregnancy," he said.

As always, when I was feeling that perhaps we suffered from lack of communication and not lack of affection, he doused my feelings. It was like pouring icy water on somebody already cold. Then he smiled diabolically. His gleeful face put me off. If I had known that he was a sadist all along, this confirmed his inhumanity at its worst.

11

POETRY WILL NOT CURE MY MAN'S SICKNESS

Here's what I discovered to my dismay: a poem and a diary entry for several days. He might have other poems or other entries, but this was what I found—the original work of my husband, Dr. Goomsay, who used to hate poetry and poets. I knew that for a year or two now he had been secretly reading more poetry, while trying to discourage me from reading or writing. He has not been happy since we started our women's creative writing club. He often asked me questions when I told him it was our meeting day—Tuesday. On some days, I did not tell him because I didn't want my spirit to be soured before our cheerful meeting. Participation in the club's activities had increased in recent times as many members sought companionship in addition to sharing writing experiences.

I am sending you the whole manuscript so that you can draw your own conclusions about his ways. He will not find it and will not have the courage to ask me about it. It should give him shame if he knew that I saw the work that he was hiding, but that should not be so. I am impressed that he now thinks and organizes his thoughts and feelings into a poem or prose entry in his diary. The swimmer's back is exposed, but he does not know and thinks he is underwater!

I can write poetry
With the pen I found on the
road. Today dawned quietly,
Like every other day.
The cock crew, but who cares?
People will wake whether the cock
Crows or not. Imagine if all cocks
Were struck mute or dead,
Who will blow the trumpet
That welcomes the sun from the east?

Today the sun will run its
course And enter the dark to re-
dress In light and come again.
Yesterday and today are the same
As today and tomorrow—everything
Enters the merry-go-round
And circles round and round one spot.
I want to remain at the center
Without moving with the corners,
Stay strong for others to run around me.

Thursday, August 3

    My wife put on a very beautiful dress to go to work today. If she wants to please me, she won't dress so gorgeously. Everything she wore was light blue: wrapper, blouse, shoes, and handbag. This woman is attractive when she wants to be. I felt like asking her to come to me. Something in me wanted her, but I couldn't bring myself to call her to spend a few more minutes with me before going to work.

    In any case, she was upbeat as if looking toward a meeting. Could that be her class or one of the many department/faculty meetings? I don't know what she's up to with her Head of Department and the Rector being so kind to her and so will watch her carefully.

    She came back late, 6 p.m. What could she be doing in her office from 9 a.m. to this time? After all, Celia did not go to school today. She cooks very fast, as if she doesn't care for the taste of the food; she then bathes and goes to bed. Before I go to bed at 9.45 p.m. after watching part of the NTA news, she is already sound asleep. She must have worked herself so tired to be so dead asleep.

Friday, August 4

More and more, Paulinus Dungs becomes more entrenched in the Tin Throne and makes it even harder for either my father or me to be the Gwom of Kwaton. A court will not help me regain it for my father. These courts favor incumbents and rarely make a ruling for the outsider, which is what my father is in this case at the moment. We are challenging Dungs and, like in boxing, the challenger has more to prove than the champion does. I left practicing medicine in the clinic to make a name in politics. That move has not done as it ought to but I expect it to strengthen our claims to the throne. I hope something will happen. My father is getting too old to be enstooled. I can ascend the throne if things work our way. A plague on Chief Paulinus Dungs and his family!

Saturday, August 5

I am going to become the executive governor of Plateau State. By the grace of God, anything can happen.

Sunday, August 6

My wife prepared very delicious food that she doesn't normally prepare for me to take to a party. She didn't even leave a plate of it for me. I inhaled the aroma and knew that it was so delicious. These are not common condiments and spices that she used to prepare the chicken soup. In my own house I deserve to have a taste of the best dish my wife prepares. Was it kind of her not to leave me part of the delicious dish? It is true that yesterday I did not eat the food she left for me on the table—not that the food was not good (I did not open the plate), but because I didn't like her silence when I came from outside. If she was waiting for me to apologize for not eating before she gave me another food, she might get a beating before she knew her rightful duty. She says one of her friends will be sent off to America after service. I go to my Church of Christ in Nigeria and before I am back she's gone to her Catholic Church. No wonder she writes so much about communion. Does she receive that their bread they

130

call *Holy Communion? I don't know. To do that she must go for confession and I don't think she has ever confessed her sins against our marriage.*

I opened her room and searched for anything that I am not aware of that she might have. Often I have found poems she wrote for that her god. Who knows whether he still writes her? My letter must have scared him. If I wanted to get rid of him, I would have put in nails, razor blades, or laced the envelope with some poison like arsenic. It is not easy to get a parcel bomb; only the State Secret Service has monopoly of it. But warning him is enough for now. I believe he won't write her anymore, write more poems for her; or not visit her again. Who knows whether she is after somebody else around here now? There must be somebody beside the Supervisor, Head of Department, and the Rector. She dresses too well for her teaching job.

I only found vitamin supplements on her bedroom table. How did she know the value of these vitamins? Is that a new discovery in literature?

Monday, August 7

My wife wore a new dress today, a jump suit as they call it. What jumping does she have to do at school? She woke early, hurriedly prepared breakfast, left mine on the dining table, and set about her makeup. Why paint her lips, rub pancake, and pencil her eyelashes with mascara? She styled her hair so fashionably. She spent a long time before the mirror in her room. When she is plotting mischief, she goes to her room. I pretended that I did not hear or see her, but she was perhaps going somewhere that her looks were so important. I almost burst into her room to ask what a housewife needs dressing so well for, but restrained myself. Or should I pull her to our bed and make love with her? She really can make herself attractive when she wants. Can't she dress like this for me after her work?

131

I watch her. It is better she feels that I don't notice her than for her to know that I am watching her. I will drive after her and see whether she heads towards the Polytechnic or takes another direction. Since she got a car with the Polytechnic's loan, she has been too quick to go out. I don't want her to tell me she is going to see one of her friends, Mrs. Esther Keko. These women spoil themselves.

Either her Ph.D. and rapid promotion have gone into her head or she is trying to attract somebody's attention. I am not going to change my mind and give her what she wants. I want her to so feel it that she will beg me to be on top of her.

Again she came late. This woman must be doing something behind my back. I will continue to watch her closely. If I catch her with another man, she will be finished—I will strangle her, but shooting will take care of both of them.

Tuesday, August 8

Went to the state police headquarters to apply for a double-barrel gun. It is not possible to get the other types of guns, the assault rifles. Armed robbery is increasing in Barkin Ladi and the entire Plateau State, and I need protection. Who will protect my children? They are all I have from the marriage, which is neither here nor there. Anna is another person's daughter. She doesn't want to leave now, but I could come home one day and she's gone to only-God-knows-where. I am not going to divorce her. She will learn to obey me in spite of her Ph.D. and poetry. I completed the gun-owning application form. That is the first step of a very long process. I will go through it, rather than buy from the underground world. I know many policemen or officers in the army will get me one if I really wanted to get it with a huge sum of money. I am rather dry now. Were it not for the little rent I receive from my abandoned clinic, I would have no money. I have kept it a secret from this woman that I get this money. If she knew that I was a property owner, she would be

132

demanding for so much money from me. Now that I tell her that I have nothing, she is able to feed the family with her earnings. If women think they are wise, we men are even wiser.

I have already paid two thousand naira to the police, and they say it is only for the application form. That is not the application fee, which has to be paid when there is initial approval for me to own a gun. After the police approval, I can then apply for the actual license to own the weapon. Nobody will notify you; instead you just have to keep going to the police station to check. I have been asked to check in three to six months for the initial approval and get ten thousand naira ready. I will pay whatever it costs. I need a gun in the house.

Wednesday, August 9

What is happening to me? As soon as Dr. Anna left the house for her so-called work—I don't now care where she goes—Mary Nuk came in. We had arranged it. I had taken Celia to school very early despite her protests that it was too early. She is not the one running my house. Mary Nuk and I played the usual way, but I was very different. I tried and tried but could not get aroused. Mary laughed at me and asked me whether I had just slept with my wife. I ignored her question. For all the months we have been making love, I did not tell her that I did not sleep with my wife. That is not her business. My house business is mine to run the way I like it. Before Mary left, I was soaked in cold sweat. I gave her five hundred naira. I hope the bitch will close her mouth and not gossip about me.

At night, I shook my wife from sleep. I knew that she did not expect me to start all of a sudden making love with her after the many months I have kept away. When I told her that I wanted her, without a word she spread herself as if it meant nothing to her. Was she asleep or awake? I couldn't tell, but I didn't care about her. I wanted to check myself; I didn't need it or her for that matter. I couldn't still go into her. She sneered *loudly at me and I knew that she was pretending to be asleep all the while. What is happening to me?*

Thursday, August 10

I dreamt. Caught the stubborn woman with Dr. Ogbe Jo, or is it Jo Ogbe, who had the face of that her supervisor and the voice of the Rector? I shot them, he on top of her. The blood splashed all over the house. The undying echoing of the gunshot woke me. I need help.

Friday, August 11

I want to smash my forehead against the ground. I want to be turbaned. What name they will give to me, I don't know—Muhammadu or Aminu should be okay. I have gone secretly to the imam to tell him my desire. I know that as Muhammadu Goomsay, I stand a better chance in life. Add politics and Islam to my life and I am on the right course to realize my goals of securing the throne. Can I still look my pastor in the eye next Sunday?

I don't know what is fantasy or truth in him. He is confused. Do you know that I did not even know when he tried to come into me? I really don't know what he is applying for a gun to do. He is turning more dangerous every passing day. I think he is fantasizing a conversion.

You'll hear more from me, later.

Annie

12

DOWN

He took the failure so far of his father's contest for the chiefdom personally. He had been thinking very far ahead—if his father won, then he would himself ascend the Tin Throne and become the Gwom of Kwaton. But for now the whole thing was a mere dream that could not be realized. He rarely talked about that issue to anybody, but once half-drunk boasted that those who outmaneuvered his father from the throne would yield to a stronger power someday and be removed. Then his father, however old, would step into the royal shoes. He cited what happened to Sultan Chido, who was selected by the sultan-selecting council only to be over-ruled by the Military Head of State, who installed Kisu in his place. Later another general who took over from him did not like the face of Kisu that was always creased with arrogance and so dethroned him for Chido. So, someday everybody is placed where he or she belongs. All he had to do for now was to establish contacts in important places. If it is God's will, it will be done. That was his fantasy. No wonder, his dream of smashing his forehead against the ground and getting turbaned! Nathan hoped to get his chiefly desire through politics and lobbying, both of which he pursued with a vengeance. Was that not why he abandoned his clinic for politics? According to him though, his patients had no money to pay and he was already owed hundreds of thousands of naira he had no hope of recovering in the dismal economy. Beside the title, doctor, which earned him respect, he was not going to make as quickly as he desired the connections that he needed to exercise power. The doctor spent too much time at work and there will be little time to meet important people outside. He had to pursue his desire with zeal. He did not care about the Hippocratic oath he took to cure and heal. He wanted name, money, and power. Attending to poor patients in the small town of Rof, close as it was to Barkin Ladi, would not make him realize his goals. He had to prioritize, he felt, on his way to the chiefdom of Kwaton or the governorship of Plateau State. What person of his education other than he would be interested in what was really a big village's throne? Gwom Goomsay! What an odd appellation! But his interests were weird and difficult to fathom rationally.

He joined the party of big guns—the All People's Congress, APC for short. It was made up of all kinds of corrupt but rich people. The rich class hijacked the mantle of the common people to appear to care for poor ones. But everybody knew they represented their own interests—further enriching themselves with the nation's wealth that ought to be used to raise the standard of living of the common folks.

The physician rubbed shoulders with very rich professional politicians who tolerated his company because he would attend to any of them, should they fall sick in the campaign tours. Many of them obese were sick anyway. And on several occasions, many really fell sick and he attended to them. He followed them like a dog, contributed neither money nor ideas to the party, apart from his doctor's expertise. Of course, his fellow party men enriched themselves in the corrupt dictatorship of the late Chaba, whom the public had not forgiven for the terror and corruption he designed and executed with steadfastness. These politicians thought that with money they could get whatever they wanted in Nigeria. They felt Nigerians had a very short memory and forgot about Chaba's atrocities as soon as he died of unnatural causes. They were mistaken in their understanding of the people who were far more intelligent than they were given credit for. The people rejected them for the Grassroots Popular Party, the GPP, which out-rigged others in the election.

Nathan sat morose. He must have been shattered by the defeat of his party, which sealed his father's contest for the local throne. He had no leverage to wield. Chief Paulinus Dungs, the current Gwom of Kwaton, was visibly during the electioneering campaign on the side of the GPP. It was said that he reluctantly entered politics because he was supposed to be neutral, but seeing his opponents publicly calling for his ouster should the APC win, he had no alternative than to join the fray. Everybody exercises survival instincts, and he was human in his decision to be political rather than be the father figure of the people. He poured in money and sent his court attendants to campaign from door to door on behalf of the GPP. The mainly farming population was promised free fertilizers, which they said the APC wanted to hoard and sell at an exorbitant price. The people of the locality, with a few exceptions, cast votes for free fertilizers—the GPP! Everybody knew that if the APC group brought home the game, they would not share it; rather they would keep it to themselves. And that too was why nobody was on its side.

For three years my doctor husband had not given me any money to supplement my salary for the upkeep of the house and I was not going to press a stone, as he pretended to be, for water. I knew the least demand for money would raise his already high temper to a flash point. He felt that I did not know that he got money from rent, and I pretended that I did not know. My monthly salary once a mere shoestring has increased considerably over the years and that has lessened the financial stress.

At daybreak, he did not take off his pajamas and change into his regular clothes. Instead, he stood by the window of the sitting room watching traffic flow in the street. You could tell that he was finding the idleness boring. I wanted to advise him again to return to his practice or bring it to Barkin Ladi itself, but that would be interpreted to be a challenge; so I didn't tell him.

Later he sat by the table with a pen and a piece of paper in front of him. I could imagine that he was trying to compose a poem or write something. However, that paper had lain white without any letter of the alphabet for days. He was still waiting for his muse whom I suspected was a tyrant. That muse must be doing to him what he had been doing to me, depriving me of freedom, pleasure, and humanity. That muse might as well hurt him, and I could care less for his woes. Maybe he felt poetry, which he so much revered, despised, and was so jealous of, would transform his condition from idleness and joblessness to a meaningful occupation.

Inattentive to my sickness, he did not ask me what was wrong. I languished in pain, my head split by incessant aches. At the same time, I had fever and often felt dizzy. His lack of concern worsened my condition. We had become two mountains under one roof; none shifted or talked to the other.

My very dear Jo:

I write to let you know that my domestic situation has gone from bad to worse. Things have never been as bad and, I suppose, I won't allow things to get to the worst. I had a horrible beating from my so-called husband three days ago even when I had a severe migraine headache. The man would have killed me were it not for the intervention of a very kind female neighbor of mine that the children had run to call to my rescue. The children were themselves appalled by his behavior. Our senior son, Dauda, came close to standing between him and me before withdrawing to go and call the kind woman. I could imagine what was going on in the boy's mind—why his mother was being so treated for no apparent reason he could think of. I believe if he felt he had the power to beat his father or stop him, he would have intervened.

The simple reason for this bestiality was that I had gone to have a blood test for malaria or typhoid without telling him. I tend to have malaria every year, but nobody is sure it is malaria and not typhoid until a blood test is done. The symptoms of the two diseases are about the same and most people, for some reasons, always think they are suffering from malaria when it could be typhoid, which is more deadly. He was angry that I went out for treatment. How can he be angry that I went out for treatment after ignoring me for so many years whenever I fell sick? He

138

certainly knew I was sick but did not think of taking me to the hospital or administering me any treatment. I was actually found to be suffering from this ailment, and given a prescription. Can you imagine that I do not even have the right over my own body to seek treatment when ignored without duly informing him first? I don't know what this type of man he is turning into. If I had told him, he would have kept quiet and walked away. Or, he would have barked "And then?" at me. I am mature enough to bear my pain alone till I seek relief on my own.

As I dressed to go to the clinic near us, he locked up all the house doors. He did not want me to leave the house and go anywhere. He yelled and shouted that I was not going anywhere as long as he was my husband and he was alive. His jealous rage had flared again. However, I knew that eventually he would swallow his threat. When I attempted to struggle out of his mad grip so as to open the door, he beat the hell out of me. He had already dragged me to the bedroom and hit my already nerve-splitting migraine-wracked head against the bed frame. I almost passed out from the pain. My husband has gone berserk. His eyes swelled and suddenly became bloodshot. He appeared possessed by some demonic spirit and foamed white at both ends of his lower mouth. He scared the hell out of me.

Our neighbor came and split us. She asked him, "Why this?" to which he did not reply. I took my handbag in which I had some money and walked out. I had to go for my treatment. He shouted that I should not come back to his house if I did not come back immediately, but I knew he was out of his mind. I would come back to the house, not to him but to my children. By the time I returned, he was asleep, I suspect, worn out by his brutish behavior.

I have been receiving treatment from the clinic and a pharmacist nearby and feel much better now. I have gone to tell my uncle, Mr. Solomon Obida, who is now a high court judge, about his favored man's bestiality. I can imagine a patriarch like him giving excuses and making it

139

look as if it should be normal for a man to beat his wife for whatever reason. His wife has aged terribly and looked older than the man who was really her senior with fifteen years. Mr. Obida promised to talk to the brute.

In any case, at this time I have to prepare to face the future squarely alone so that I can at least live for my children who are still very small. I have told his elder brother that enough is enough. He tells me that I should be patient with the man who still claims to be my husband. For how long can one be patient with a madman on the loose? He pretends to apologize but I have not uttered a word to him, even when he talks to me he gets no response. I am just dumb to him just as I am still completely dumbfounded.

He got himself into politics and since things did not work out well for him, he thinks I should be the punching bag for his woes. I advised him to do something meaningful with his training, but he did not listen to me. I am not responsible for his failure, but he is taking it out on me because he thinks I am weak. I am not weak; it is the culture that thinks women are weak.

He has never been, nor will ever be, a man of the people. How can such a person ever think of winning support of the very people he treats with disdain or too poor for him to treat? I told him when he was beating me that his behavior was worse than that of an illiterate.

You see, Jo, all that he is doing is to destabilize me so that I will no longer advance fast in my career. He thinks I have advanced too far already. I don't think that he even wants me to stand still; he wants me to retrogress. If I stand still as a Dr. Goomsay with him, that will still be too much for his pride to swallow—if in a gathering somebody called the name, either of us could be meant. He saw it as an equality that he was not ready to concede to me. At one time he had asked me to put "Mrs." after my Dr. to be "Dr. (Mrs.) Anna Goomsay. I asked him whether he put "Mr." after his. Since he could not answer my question, he never bothered

140

me about it again. He had no way of stripping me of either my Ph.D. or my chief lectureship. The earlier he reconciles himself to my status, the better for him. He may beat me but I will no longer leave him alone. I will strike back blow for blow until he leaves me alone.

When you come to Bukuru this time, be careful. Bukuru, as you know, is so close to Barkin Ladi. The man has been on the hunt for any piece of information concerning you and me. Thank God, all my poems and letters are in my office under lock and key. It seems he no longer feels that his letter to you has worked the way he anticipated. I don't know what the status of his application to own a gun is. He might already have a gun in the house. If I find it, I'll take it and throw it away into some hidden ravines in the outskirts of town. Just be careful. Keep the date of your coming here known to only me and to nobody else here. I never in my life thought that I would be living this kind of nightmarish life that I nonchalantly chose without the faintest hint of this cruelty.

You are bound to feel horrible about my situation since I know you care for me. I'll tell you all later when you arrive. I am trying to cope with life as it is, and I am sure I will be all right. July seems so far away. Take good care of yourself as I do of myself here.
Love,
Annie

13

CAREER HIGH

Thank God I came to teach at The State Polytechnic. I have already exceeded the expectations of my wildest dream. In just about a decade I rose from Lecturer II to Chief Lecturer. My department head said I worked hard, but I thought I was just doing what I was hired for in teaching, writing, and doing community service. If I had a better atmosphere at home, indeed a room that was truly my own, I would have done more in writing and outreach programs. Modest had been my efforts, but I could do much more in more auspicious circumstances.

I had risen from being a member of the Student/Staff Disciplinary Committee to being its Chairperson. I often wondered what discipline I had to judge others in matters of discipline. Many female students often reported male lecturers, who harassed them for sex and when they resisted were failed in the courses they took despite their performance. The departments of Mathematics and Chemistry were the most notorious. When a male lecturer wanted a female student and she declined his advances, he conspired with other male lecturers in the department to make her flunk their examinations and get a D grade in his. In this way the accused lecturer would look even generous compared to the others in the department. What tricks some men play!

The Rector, Professor Emmanuel Semshak, an elderly man, took these accusations seriously and wanted them thoroughly investigated. There were serious and frivolous cases, and I would be the last person in the committee to let a serious student or a responsible male lecturer to be punished. But abusive lecturers or mischievous students also had to be taught a lesson for responsible relationships in the campus. I noticed that the female students worked hard and generally proved themselves as intelligent as the male ones. I was happy that the Women's Creative

Writing Group and the NOW group have disseminated the gospel of hard work for women throughout The State Polytechnic and the Barkin Ladi area. The progress made by the women's groups in a few years had been astounding.

I became somehow too well known in the campus, Barkin Ladi, and the entire State for Nathan's comfort. I had been elected as the staff representative in The State Polytechnic's Governing Council, which met about three times a year to discuss policy matters of the institution. I was also elected national vice president of the National Organization for Women in Abuja. We had as our project, during our two-year tenure, mobilizing rural women and their daughters about literacy/education and the pros and cons of female circumcision. Fortunately, the practice was not common in our Plateau State, but we still enlightened women about the practice, which we wanted stopped for medical and emotional reasons. Our agenda was publicized in the media. National newspapers often reported our activities and mentioned me in them. On some occasions, the papers published my photograph that was very charitable to my looks.

My husband took this exposure of not only my name but also my photograph in a negative way. He brought home the Sunday issue of *The Guardian* that had my interview and photographs.

"Who is this?" he asked as he spread out the paper before me.

It was different photographs taken when I was being interviewed. "Can't you see how commonplace you are making yourself?" he again asked.

"What's wrong in my talking about women's education?" I asked back.

"And your pictures are part of women's education?" he retorted sarcastically.

He was breathing very hard. He had worked himself up again. My visibility, or call it popularity, was again the root of this outburst.

143

"Don't you know that popular women sleep around? Don't you know that the men who make the appointments need something in return?"

"Are you telling me that women don't deserve appointments in their right? Or you are telling me that every intelligent woman is a prostitute?"

In the course of our altercation, he called me Miss Feminist. Of course, I responded by calling him Mr. Patriarch. My quick retort made him stop playing with the feminist label.

Our creative writing group successfully lobbied for the Association of Nigerian Authors, the national umbrella organization of writers, to meet in Bukuru. We beat Lagos and Ibadan that always wanted to dominate everything in Nigeria. We also beat Kaduna that saw itself as the only truly northern Nigerian town. We prepared adequately for this annual convention. We were able to get the University of Bukuru as venue of the convention to partly sponsor it. The State Polytechnic, through the intervention of our women's Creative Writing Club, gave money toward the successful hosting of the convention. The Plateau State Government also gave us money. We thus had a fat purse from which to make participants very comfortable. Private businessmen and companies in the State assisted. We never knew Plateau people could be so generous towards the arts. Out of this money, we published an anthology of Plateau writers with poems, short stories, and short plays of many of our young women represented.

We lavishly treated the guests from other states with free accommodation and meals. Buses were there with drivers to take people on tours of Bukuru and the State. Our secondary school girls performed two plays that my colleagues wrote specially for the occasion. It should have been one of the most attended and exciting ANA annual conventions ever, a point *The Standard* harped upon.

Though the convention took a lot of me physically, I was more than thrilled by its success. Who ever thought we could host a national convention successfully? Some of us women were already thinking the next thing was to bring the national conference of NOW to Plateau State. After all, the experience of ANA should help us do even better with another convention.

Then, very unexpectedly, I was appointed Executive Secretary of the State University Establishment Committee. Plateau State wanted to have its own university like Nasarawa and there was talk of either converting an established tertiary institution such as a polytechnic or college of education or starting somewhere from scratch. You could call it state rivalry in the country since Nasarawa, a new State, had one now and it was considered a shame if Plateau State, a much older State, had none. Most of the southern states already had one each and many in the north had established universities as well. Kogi and Benue were already about to start theirs. Plateau must have felt it had to follow suit rather than be left behind. Everyone talked about the importance of education. The federal university in the State, the University of Bukuru, was not enough. The State Polytechnic granted National Diplomas, which could not compare with higher degrees. And so, it was announced that I had been appointed the Executive Secretary of the Committee to execute the establishment of a Plateau State University. The assignment, to me, was simple. We needed a state university to have more of our people in higher institutions of learning. It would be better for the government to spend its money on education than have it squandered away through reckless spending and corruption.

Days after this announcement, the civil war in my home intensified. The announcement fully covered on television and newspapers carried the details of the members of the Committee and their qualifications. Nathan got really furious that I was going to work with the Committee's Chairman, Paul Zidik, a handsome, brilliant, and Oxford-educated professor from the University of Bukuru.

145

To my surprise, Nathan went to complain that he did not want his wife in the position, since they had young children. That was a lie because they were teenagers and not babies. However, he must have given other reasons too. In any case, the Deputy Governor was very surprised and even mentioned it to his colleagues, who described the man as funny for his response. He told Nathan, as I learnt later, that it was for him to convince his wife to reject the appointment but that she had already accepted and would be sworn in the next day. Nathan stayed away from the swearing-in ceremony and disappeared from home for two days. He said that he was traveling to Abuja to interview for a job, an excuse I knew was a lie. Fortunately, Celia was more experienced in helping with house chores and my boys had become boarders in their secondary schools.

The Chairman of the State University Establishment Committee, Professor Zidik, had to lead a delegation to several universities in the country and, if we considered it necessary, to two outside Nigeria. I was one of the five members of the delegation. An autonomous body under the direct supervision of the Governor, the Committee was close to power. My responsibility as the administrative head involved tours and a lot of power. I had cars, drivers, and there was the possibility of my playing a very important role in the institution once the university was established. When I told Nathan about my responsibilities as the Executive Secretary, he went into the bedroom as he banged the door. He became restless for days because of the many trips and late nights involved in the appointment. His jealousy intensified, but he knew he could not stop me. Many who knew us came to congratulate him as well as myself, for being appointed as the Executive Secretary of the committee. But he squirmed, as if I was going to leave him because I was running the state committee. The day before we left for the visitations, he sulked as usual, grumbling out loud nothing I could decipher from his mumbles. He was very suspicious of the highly respected Chairman, as if he were again already or going to be my lover.

At the University of Lagos, the vice-chancellor received us in his big and heavily furnished office. After a few pleasantries and tea, he directed us to his deputy vice-chancellor for Academic Affairs, who, he said, would provide us with the details of the academic programs. He telephoned somebody that we assumed was our next contact in the university and asked his secretary to take us to him. And who other than Professor Jonah Ogbe received us! We stared at each other for a halfminute but would not allow our long established friendship to interfere with this official business. I was expecting him to visit me in a few months, but that was another matter. He had been appointed to the position only three weeks earlier and was still studying what his position entailed. He thus had not had time to write me about his appointment. Things had also been moving at such a fast pace at my end that I had not written him the past few months either. I congratulated him before the rest of my delegation.

"Sit down," he said, pointing to comfortable chairs on another side of the office.

I suspect the vice-chancellor did not inform him before today that the university was expecting our Committee. However, he provided us documents, which he asked his secretary to copy for us. We asked him questions about different departments and what he felt a new university should learn from an old one such as theirs. Having been in the system for so long and a professor, he knew much about organizational and curricular matters of a university.

"Start with departments whose personnel you can easily recruit and plan ahead for relevant departments whose staff are scarce. Start slowly but aggressively and with time you will find expansion easy to handle," he explained.

He promised that the University of Lagos would be delighted to second to us three professors to help establish three faculties, if we made a formal request and that other personnel exchange and linkage agreements could be worked out. This would include the training of our academic and administrative staff. In exchange, the University of Lagos's research area could extend to Plateau State. I knew he made those generous offers for my sake.

Before I returned, Nathan had learnt that our committee visited Lagos, among other places, where he knew Dr. Jo Ogbe was. He must have prepared to harass me on this but looked for a way to start a quarrel almost as soon as I came in.

"I didn't know you were going to Lagos? Why did you confuse me with Yerwa, which you didn't even go to?" he asked.

"We went to Yerwa, Zaria, and Lagos. In fact, Lagos was a late addition when we learnt that the vice-chancellor of Ibadan University was away for two weeks."

"And that served you well."

"I went purely for my official assignment," I explained.

"Tell the fool and he will believe you."

I was in a no-win situation in this type of argument and so went to my room to lie down. He was rattled by my new responsibilities and feared I could be appointed into a bigger office. I overhead him murmuring sarcastically about women as heads of institutions, but I had to ignore him and patriarchs of his kind.

The Committee had an office given us by the Governor, who offered to give us official quarters if we wanted. Both the Chairman and I declined and the other members had to do the same. Nathan was already so jealous and I did not want to make things worse. I did accept though, a policeman to guard our house and to accompany me to the office. We, earlier on, decided that, for the time being, visiting the older Nigerian universities was enough. After the establishment of the State University, its officials could tour the United States and Great Britain to observe firsthand how universities were run abroad. I knew that traveling abroad at that time would have driven Nathan crazy, with his unnecessary jealousy.

148

14

SHAME

After every effort to discourage me in my profession failed, Nathan sought avenues to punish me emotionally and psychologically. He always invented new ways of shocking me, and prepared as I was for his erratic actions, I never envisaged the extent to which he could go.

He had wanted to punish me by neglecting me in every way to the extent of abandoning his marital responsibilities. Not that I cared about that; he was also punishing himself. After my efforts to inflame him failed, he no longer moved me—he was like a log beside me in bed. He had turned from me for months, believing that I would someday beg him to make love with me. He knew what he was doing.

According to the male-favored customs he subscribed to, a man could have affairs outside—have as many concubines and girlfriends—while the woman at home would be expected to remain loyal to an unfaithful husband. Some men marry other wives and settle them in other apartments where they spend much of their free time. The housewife becomes a hostage to patriarchal customs. Many educated wives of even so-called educated men who are also Christians have been sexually starved for months or even years to the delight of their husbands. We women keep this a secret from each other, and only among very close and old friends do we divulge this. We do not want others to know the extent of our marital woes and so cover our emotional wounds from the public. Many dress lavishly and smile without cause to cover up the wounds. Imagine my telling Debra and Josephine what I am going through! I am sure they would ask me to walk out or publicly get a lover. I do not seek any of those alternatives yet because of my children. My friend around, Esther Keko, suspected for long that I was not happy, but was rebuffed by Nathan when she tried to ask him whether I was well. In fact, he already feels that

149

I have told her all about him and doesn't want to see her. The last time she visited me, he went out as soon as she entered without greeting her. I have not told her the details of my woes, bad as they are. I know she suspects that I am not happy with him, but that's all she knows to this point.

Some men go as far as boasting about their sexual exploits outside to hurt the housewives the more. Many helpless women who lack the fortitude and the dignity to counter patriarchal tyranny with their free will go down on their knees to report to relatives or friends of the man to intervene so that their husbands could make love with them. Of course, the husbands would be doing a favor making love with their humiliated wives! This will be a weapon such men would always wield whenever it pleased them. I will never buy this one-sided solution that some neglected and pressed wives choose.

I switched off my sexual desires not only to cope with the condition but also to defeat tyranny and sadism. If he waited for me to beg, he would be waiting for Godot; and Godot would never arrive. Even if I had been awake or conscious the very night he recorded that he wanted me, I would have pushed him away. In that instance, he got enough selfinflicted humiliation.

After I surpassed his expectation of what he expected a woman to endure, he started to be fretful about everything I did. If I dressed well, he asked for where I was going. He came close to deliberately soiling my new dress, but I escaped the milk he splashed after me. If I put on makeup, he wondered out loud whether a housewife should be made up so alluringly to work where there were many men. I deliberately stayed long at work to have the space and the right atmosphere to write. If students came in too frequently after my office hours, I went to a quiet section of the library to work. I wanted space into which the tyrant could not intrude or poison with malice. Of course, I participated as actively as I could in the activities of the Women's Creative Writing Club and the State branch of NOW. In fact, once the children went to boarding schools, I threw myself fully into teaching and my two club activities. I was home only when I had to be.

He must be looking for clues as to how I came to be appointed as the Executive Secretary of the State University Establishment Committee. To him, a woman can achieve nothing without giving herself to men. That false notion must intensify his jealousy, since I wanted to work hard and that meant staying long in the office. Though I was in a polytechnic, which emphasized technology, I tried to keep myself abreast with the arts and humanities and read as many new publications as I could lay my hands on.

I wanted to write more poetry and articles, I wanted to be free. I wrote myself into freedom from dependence, I wrote myself into sanity. At home he was all over me simply to disturb my sanity. I could have no peace at home. He seized every opportunity to disengage me from a propitious writing mood. If I sat before a book, he asked me to do something.

"Bring me water!" he would command.

I complied at first when I did not want him to say that I was not deferring to him because I then had a doctoral degree. Later I ignored his commands. But his outbursts for my disobedience and shouts killed the poem brewing in my head. He was quick to ask me what I was drinking when he saw me once taking medications. Was he afraid that I would kill myself? He did not know me. I could not choose the path of cowardice or any other that would shame my children. I was resolved to triumph over his evil contrivances. I had learnt that from experience and from Debra. I had grown so forgetful that I often drove past where I should be going. Now and then I took the wrong turn. It was the day that I drove past our house that I realized that I had to keep myself sane. I was already going beyond the edge and there was the possibility of falling into the abyss. If he wanted me to be out of my mind, he would rejoice at what he had achieved. But I would not give him the comfort of joy over my demise.

151

I had begun eating under compulsion for months. It was as if my stomach were the proverbial bottomless pit that could not be filled. I took snacks, ate between meals, discriminated against no types of food. I drank so much Coke. I also took alcohol, especially sweet wine, which was deceptively strong. Don Simon and Pink Lady were my favorites. Soon I could see for myself the effects of my voracious lifestyle. My size-14 dresses were too tight for me to wear, and if I squeezed myself inside them, I felt uncomfortable. I must have reached size-17/18 in six months!

Colleagues observed that I had put on so much weight. A female colleague, who had not seen me for some weeks, met me in the library, took me aside and winked mischievously at me. Then she asked,

"Should I congratulate you? When will you be due?"

"For what?" I asked.

With talks and gossips in the campus always about promotion, I was really at a loss about her question. I had been promoted only a year ago to Chief Lecturer and that was the highest I could reach. I had also been made Acting Dean of General Studies, which had grown from a department to a division. My former head of department had retired. I was still productive but for self-improvement and not for promotion. Or was it for a campus appointment that I was not yet aware of? It might be my acting appointment had been made substantive.

"Come on, am I blind? Don't you see your body? Isn't it two in one?"

I understood, and told her I was not pregnant. My colleague was not satisfied, from her "Okay-o!" When I had been pregnant for four months, nobody in the campus noticed it until it disappeared.

Much as I wanted to at times, I could not read or write at home. My office became a sanctuary and a temple, where my muse communed with me. Because my man ransacked my room, I kept my books and poems in the office. He must still be stealing into my room whose key he kept. He fully asserted his domineering authority in that way.

152

One day I was not feeling fine and stayed home. He had fidgeted around me for some time, even asked me for once why I did not go to work since I taught that day of the week. I answered him that I was not feeling fine and needed to rest. He appeared most uncomfortable with my staying at home to rest.

"Who will teach your class for you?" he asked.

"Don't worry. The students have covered much of the syllabus already and can miss this class and still be all right," I said.

"Why can't you go and tell your Secretary to tell the students that you are sick?" he asked.

That was not a bad suggestion. However, I was just too weak to drive to the office and I told him I just wanted to rest. After all, I told him, missing one class that could easily be made up for was no big loss. I would have been surprised if he chose to go to tell the departmental secretary that I was sick and that the students should be dismissed for that day. But I never got a pleasant surprise from him.

He went in, took his car keys and went outside. I thought he was driving out to my department to tell the secretary that I was sick. What a sudden change, I felt. But he soon came back, stood by the door for a moment, and then went into the bedroom. I watched him without his knowing.

About a quarter of an hour later there was a soft knock on the door. The knock was repeated two more times and in the same feeble way by a person I thought must be very civil. I went to the door, opened it; and there stood a lady by the threshold. She looked like a rural person who had just come to town from her demeanor. She tied a brightly colored wrapper and wore a brown blouse over it. She wore no scarf and her hair was not styled or plaited. She wore slippers. I measured her from head to toe.

"Is Dr. Goomsay in?" she asked.

"Which one?" I asked back.

153

"The man," she said.

"Who are you?" I asked.

"Madam, don't you know me?" she asked back.

"No!" I answered.

"Dr. Goomsay is my uncle," she explained.

"What's your name?" I asked.

"Mary Nuk," she answered.

I knew I had caught the thief. This must be the same Mary Nuk of the diary entries. Her voice was trembling. She withdrew her foot on the doormat backwards. She was preparing for a retreat.

"What do you want him for?" I asked.

"I want to greet him," she replied.

I thought of allowing her in to watch how he would receive his secret niece, but decided against creating a scene. I knew what she was saying was a lie. If she were his niece, I would have known her. But he had only a senior brother, no other brother or sister with a grownup woman for daughter. Where did this niece surface from in his family? If he slept with this sort of woman to deride me, then I have an opportunity to pay back.

"Mary Nuk has no uncle in this house. Go away. Don't let me see you here again," I told her, and she, visibly trembling, turned to go away. As soon as she was out in the street, I heard him cough and move in the bed. I don't know whether he knew that his mistress had come or not. However, from his fretting this morning, I could tell now that he was expecting her at a set time—11 o'clock in the morning. And even if he knew that I was talking to her, he did not know how to deal with the situation and so decided to hide in bed. I went to him in the bedroom and shook him from his tricky sleep.

"Your niece is here," I announced to him.

He got up and came to the parlor after me. I took his hand and led him to the door and pointed in the direction of Mary Nuk still not gone far away. He saw her clearly and withdrew from the door to go back to the bedroom. I stood, emboldened by a new spirit, to stop him from leaving. I wanted to confront him headlong.

"You are always suspecting me, and yet here's Mary Nuk. Is she your niece? Have you no shame? Has my "nephew" ever come to this house? You must have been doing this for a long time. Tell me, who is she, your niece with whom you sleep when I am out or who?"

"Don't ask me. I don't know," he said as he pushed me aside to pass to the bedroom.

"I have caught you at your dirty tricks," I shouted at him. I felt I had proved my point. He now knew that I had caught him, known the rustic woman he secretly met to despise me. If he liked, he could continue with the relationship with his mistress.

I was not prepared, could never have been prepared for the next shocking and shameful act of my husband. When I wanted to bring in my young niece, he resisted the idea. I had felt too lonely in the house with him alone after my two kids went to boarding schools. I explained that I needed help.

"Help for what?" he thundered.

"How do you expect me to do everything in the home, run every errand, work, wash plates and clothes, and still do my work? I asked. "You are not bringing your sister's daughter into my house," he shouted.

But I had made up my mind to do what I thought would be good for me, whether he approved of it or not. I had already told my sister that I would like to have her daughter live with me and she agreed. I brought in Celia, my niece. She was soon registered in a day secondary school in town. She went to the afternoon session, from 1 to 6 p.m. I thus left for work and Nathan took her to school, while I brought her back from school at the end of the day. I continued with this routine even as Executive Secretary of the State University Committee.

Things appeared normal all the while, as I could tell. Until one day, alone with Celia, she told me what dumbfounded me. My husband used to call her, once I left for work, to come to him so that he could help her with her homework. Even when she said that she had none, he still insisted on her coming to him. My husband never one day asked our children about their homework when they lived with us. He would ask Celia to sit on his lap, raising her dress. He would touch the innocent virgin girl at her most private parts. After he pulled down her underwear and sat her on his lap behaving sheepishly, the girl could sense something weird in his behavior. From then on, she ran outside whenever he called her for the homework assistance.   "Sister," she told me, "Daddy has been pulling down my dress and putting me on his lap."

My mind went to Mama Oyewole's son Peter, whom we called Daddy because he stole all the looks of his father. We were neighbors and Daddy sometimes ironed my husband's clothes.

"I have to tell her mother," I said.

"No, our Daddy," Celia said.

I felt cold and so disgusted that I did not know what to do immediately. I did not want to confront the devil directly. He wanted to spoil the girl to humiliate me, and he did not care about his name. He might have tried unsuccessfully to go into the girl. Could you imagine if she were deflowered and impregnated? Enraged as I was, I decided to act quietly without betraying my knowledge.

The following morning, I took Celia to his brother and asked her to tell her story, which she did in graphic detail. Barnabas Goomsay felt ashamed and shocked. He said that lack of work was no excuse for his junior brother to do what he did.

"An idle mind is the devil's workshop, but this is inexcusable. I will talk to him," he told me.

156

From that day on, I took over the responsibility of taking Celia to and from school. The girl sat in my office until it was time for her school and I then I took her there. I took a lunch bag for both of us to the office. We came back in the evening together as usual. I avoided leaving her alone with the man metamorphosed into a hyena in the house. I kept quiet and did not confront him over the issue. I wanted him to put things together and to realize that I then knew what he had been doing with my niece, even before his brother would scold him for his disgraceful conduct. A week passed before he came to me as I watched television alone. Since it was his practice to spy on me and not keep me company, I waited for his next move.

"I am sorry," he said.

He had never said sorry to me before and might not be used to saying sorry to others, so the words came out of his mouth with great difficulty.

"Sorry for what?" I asked.

I suspected the direction he was going, but with him I could never be totally sure. A master in the art of surprising acts, I wanted him to come out with what he was sorry for. You never know what a spy could be sorry for. He had caused me a lot of distress. He was a thief caught in the act and could not deny the shameful thing. He knew that my niece had told me by now with our going out together in the morning and leaving him alone. It seemed his brother had already reproached him. He had to say something to me on this issue.

"I have a problem," he said.

I kept mute. I wanted him to say what was on his mind.

"I can't have an erection," he stammered out.

I wanted to ask him how he knew he couldn't have an erection if he had not slept with me for almost eleven months, if his attempt to punish me through starvation had not backfired; but I did not. Then he told me a story, which only stupid people would believe, to rationalize his disgraceful act before one who could be his own daughter.

"I went to a herbalist in Azare to check about it, this lack of erection. Many men who had similar problems had gone to him and he had cured them. I learnt from our talk in the club that some of us had had a similar problem. They are all fine now and many have impregnated their wives. Since every man had good results, I went to Hassan. His place was filled with men with similar problems as mine. He gave me some herbs to bathe with, others to put in a bottle of gin and drink. He recommended that I try fondling a virgin girl to regain my erection before coming to you. I was only preparing myself for you. I didn't mean to spoil her, I was only trying to have an erection," he said lamely.

"What do you do with an erection with a girl on your lap?" "I didn't mean to," he retorted and paused without completing the statement.

"What type of herbalist was teaching you to molest small girls? If my niece whom you didn't want to be here in the first place were not here, whom would you have tried your stupid medicine on?" He stood very small before me.

"And if you got the erection, what would you have done with it?" I asked.

He wiped his face with a handkerchief, as if that would wipe off the shame. Sweat dripped down his brows. By the corner of his chin was a light black birthmark or splotch I had not noticed before in him. He was becoming ugly by the minute. He tried to stammer out some words, but I would not allow him to talk. I wanted to strip him of his patriarchal superiority complex, which he had exercised for too long.

"Are you telling me that you, a British-trained medical doctor who used to direct a clinic, went to an illiterate herbalist to treat you for perhaps a self-inflicted condition?" I asked.

I did not wait for his answer. As teenagers in school at Fiala, I had heard stories of weak men whose erections were made possible by

158

medicine men, but could not cool down and were later taken to hospital for surgery.

"Remember you even denied my pregnancy as yours? First, it was your "niece" Mary Nuk who stole to you, now it is my real niece you have been trying to violate. I do not accept your explanation for this dastardly act," I told him, and left the room. He was incapacitated.

15

SEEING THROUGH A NEW MASK

My husband must have realized that he had gone too far in trying to ensure my total submission to his lordship. He knew that the oppressed could become so desperate as to take any measures necessary to free themselves of their crushing burden. He thus did not know what form it would take, but feared my inevitable rebellion against him. He had already had a foretaste of what I could do in my silent resistance to his cruel dominion. I believe that shook him. Yes, my simple silence rattled him. He now appeared ready for a truce in our domestic war that had raged from the very first days of marriage. I had experienced nothing of a honeymoon. It was as if I had to marry him and he had to marry me for considerations other than love-related. Did I not cry alone in bed on what was supposed to be a delightful night for any newly wed? After the reception which took place in the afternoon, he went with his fellow doctors to the club to have a good time and came back late, falling asleep on a couch in the sitting room. And the next morning he laid out for me rules I had to obey as a housewife. I should not make friends. I should not join any women's association. I should not go out after dark. He rattled them on. But that was a very long time ago, when I expected good feelings from him. The pity is that there has been no change for the better—the leopard cannot shed its spots. Our relationship has not just gone from bad to worse, but in the last three years plummeted to its lowest nadir, the worst ever.

I thought bringing himself to apologize for his misbehavior with Celia should have chastened him. I rejected his apology but watched his every act the days and weeks following. To me, his words of apology needed to be preceded or followed by acts of penitence. Was he going to be a changed man for good? Why should I not forgive, if I saw that he was really sorry in deed and would be an amiable husband to me from henceforth? I would lavish him with love if he showed concern and care for me. After all, everyone can make a mistake. At the same time there is room for redemption. I go to church on Sundays, and although I am not very religious in a conventional sense, I do believe that sacrifice can lead to atonement. I looked on and waited for Nathan to work towards earning my forgiveness. He must also be expecting me to change so as to close the big divide between us.

During this period he did not taunt me about my extra-curricular activities. He seemed to accept my women's creative writing club and NOW membership. I told him when I was going to meetings and he did not query me for spending too much time outside. He even asked how the State University Establishment Committee was going and I told him we were about handing over to an Implementation Sub-Committee of which I was Chair. The State Government was thinking of appointing an acting vice-chancellor to start the university and run it for two to three years before a substantive officer would be appointed. He grimaced, as if afraid I could be appointed to the position, but showed no temperament at this time of one who would oppose it. I was happy that at last the relationship was going to overcome its problems. We did not turn from each other in bed, but each of us might have been disappointed at the times we made love—if that was what we did. It was awkwardly done as he was never strong enough and I was not ready in spirit. We were still far away from love or what others described as marital bliss. We would get to familiarize ourselves with each other all over again after so many years of tension and heartaches. I still wrote in the office and basically followed what had become my routine over the years.

About two months had passed of, at best, a lukewarm atmosphere in the house following his lack of erection incident. As had happened so often before, he never sat beside me for us to watch a television program or movie together. We sat opposite each other. I had given up trying to be close to him after he asked me whether I was a cat that I wanted to be all over him. He got up whenever I sat beside him, and after some time I gave up. He needed his own space to himself and I also from then on wanted mine to myself. He was used though to spying on me. He tried to check what I read or watched—the same philosophy that informed his secret reading of my poems. He wanted to know my mind and feelings by indirect means without any effort to assist me to fulfill them. Rather, he would work against my progress and happiness.

He made me feel like a whore one night that I watched a video movie that I had borrowed from my friend Esther. She had told me about this exciting movie that I needed to watch. I even nursed the idea of watching it first and then inviting him to watch it with me. In former times he would not accept my invitation, but with his seeming change, he could be interested. In any case, I wanted to enjoy it and still give him the chance to see it if it was really as wonderful as I had been told. There I was enraptured by the story of this couple. There was nothing obscene in it, but he broke in at the very time the couple were undressing for bed and swathing themselves in one sheet to either sleep or make love. It was subtle.

"Is this the type of thing a housewife should be watching?" he asked thunderously.

I was amazed at the violence in his voice, hoarse from unnecessary strain.

"What's wrong in a man and his wife sleeping naked and making love? Isn't it normal?" I asked.

He did not answer my questions. Maybe he did not know what he was supposed to do as a husband. He dashed straight to the television VCR set and pressed the STOP/EJECT button. I left for bed without further talking to him that night. In bed we faced opposite sides again, and he talked angrily to the wall for much of the night before I fell asleep. When he was out the following day, I watched the entire movie. I did not want him to prevent me from the experience I sought. I believe this adversely affected our relationship that had been improving gradually.   It came as a surprise to me one evening because I thought we were becoming a happy couple at last. Some days after his apology, he sat by me for up to fifteen minutes. He did not say anything nasty to annoy me as he used to. He even tried to joke with me. This was so strange because he was like a toad jumping about in daytime and I looked out for what was pursuing it. It surely would come out sooner or later.

"I won't mind reading your poems and commenting on them for you," he offered.

He still did not see the sense in calling my name before talking to me. He was used to talking into space and he expected me to hear. Here was a medically trained man who secretly took to reading poetry and who knew that I had a Ph.D. in literature and wrote poetry. He had not one day asked me to give him a book of poetry to read. He had not asked me to look at what he was scribbling secretly. Now he offered to read my poems and comment on them for me. I almost answered instantly that he could. But for close to fourteen years with this man, he carefully plotted his moves before venturing out. He was not a spontaneous man, and that accounted for the tall fence separating us.

On reflex, I answered on the negative. I could see through his new mask of a gentleman into an ogre that would devour or torment me, once I submitted to his power.

"No, thanks. My poems are private and I want to keep them so till I want them published. Maybe before then, I might change my mind and ask you to read what I want you to read of mine; but for now, No!" I felt he wanted to be fully aware of what I wrote. He could encourage me in more ways in my writing than his reading my poems. If he made home hospitable and afforded me the time, he would be helping me a great deal. Couldn't he help me in writing by doing some of the chores in the house that many men were doing? Why should he not put his food on the table and take the plates to the sink after he was done with eating? There was much he could do to give me more time and space to write. But I suspected he wanted to censor my emotions and thoughts on paper to be better able to control me according to his anachronistic customs. I wanted to maintain full sovereignty over my feelings and thoughts as over my body.

He did not show any disappointment at my refusal, but murmured that he already knew the scandalous things I was writing anyway. "Whether you give them to me or not, I will somehow read them," he said.

"Maybe someday when they are published," I told him. His mask had already fallen off his face! He had his scheming ways and he thought he was very smart. But ignorant, he did not know that for years now I no longer kept my poems in the house. Instead I had them under lock and key in my office where I had the privacy to write without any harassment.

If he wanted to show affection, he always did it in a very weird manner that turned me off. There was the day that I took a measured dose of cough medication with the bottle-accompanied plastic tiny cup. I think it is called a vial, but I am not sure. After I had done and washed the cup,

163

he asked me to bring him water to drink with it. He had been watching me without my knowing.

"This is for taking medication, not drinking water," I told him. As a doctor he knew that very well. So he must be out of his mind or be up to something by his strange request.

"You know that I know that," he replied.

I looked at him. He stood stern, waiting for me to bring him water with the equivalent of three tablespoons.

"Just wait, you'll get your water," I told him.

I went to the kitchen, took a neat glass from the cupboard, rinsed it, and gave him water in it. I watched him for his reaction to my blatant disobedience.

He drank the full glass. He would have taken a dozen or more of these spoonfuls for the same amount of water.

"What's so special in that small cup that I can't drink with it?" he asked.

I walked away. That was one of those his questions that deserved no response from me.

Once he came to me while I was writing. I ignored him. But on this occasion, he made no effort to spy on me. He kept a good distance from my table.

"If I come to you, soon I'll be in one of your poems," he told me.

"My poetry is about my life," I said to him.

"But why do you write about me?"

"I write about what affects me. I express my feelings and thoughts. There are many intersections here and there," I told him.

"But I have not crossed any lines you drew," he said.

He failed to understand how he adversely affected my feelings all the years. In any case, he feared or revered the power of poetry, the durability of writing. As the perpetrator of pain, he would rather not be on paper to provide evidence against his person.

Nathan would never lend himself to any form of simple prediction. His habits were still erratic and he remained unchanged. In him I could see a man struggling to make up his mind one way or another but never deciding on a firm position. I used almost all my salary to feed the family and take care of the children's boarding and tuition fees. He provided no money for even the food he ate. Fortunately, we were only three mouths and five when the boys were at home during their vacation. Either he was too proud or did not care because he did not ask how I was able to feed him and the children. He must feel that I earned much with my chief lecturer position and the recent government appointment. Gone were the days when he refused the food I gave to him for one flimsy reason or another.

In the village wives sought to please their husbands by way of their stomachs by preparing for them the most delicious dish possible. Most times, in the polygamous household, the wife who cooked for the man slept with him that day. The man's heart went for who best pleased his appetite for delicacies—a double treat for the man who was lord! Whenever a man wanted to hurt his wife, he would refuse to eat the woman's food. And that was despite the fact that he had not given her money to buy the foodstuffs. Plus the tedious hours the woman had spent by the fireside after her own day's work and chores. The food and sexoutlawed woman still had to beg her man to eat her food.

Nathan practiced the customs that pleased him. At the very beginning of our marriage, when he used it as a weapon against me, I felt bad and unwanted. I wanted to be desired in every way, food and body. But that time passed a long time ago. Since he did not show any interest in whatever I did, I hardened. Experience in marriage changes one from softness to hardness under certain circumstances. What I used to fret over, now looked at with a cold eye. Even when he provided the money for food and refused the meal for being late or other senseless reason, I took it away and ate it. There were many times I heated the same soup, put it in a different plate or re-arranged it in the same plate, and gave it back to him—he ate the very food he had rejected the previous day! I no longer had time to pine over the displeasure of my tormentor.

Now that he did not provide for the family's upkeep, he did not wield his food rejection weapon often and totally. If he refused to eat after opening the plate when he asked for that very dish, it did not matter to me. Let him starve himself, if he so wished. I suspected he still got his rent and ate at the club. So, after putting his food on the table, I left and checked after about an hour to remove the plates whether he ate or not. Sixteen years of marriage and we still did not eat together. One of his early bombshells was refusing to eat with me. He told me pointedly that he wanted to eat alone. I had thought that marriage would involve sharing, a form of communion that eating together was part of. But my lord husband would not eat with a woman, even if she should be his wife who prepared the food. An unreasonable man for that, I feel. What if the wife, who is also cook, so gets angry and decides to poison the food for her lord? After some time, there was no real effort on his side to warm up to me. He was still his rigid self, unbending in his habits. He tried to hurt me in as many possible ways as he could device to please himself. The season of what I thought would remove the divide between us was still-borne.

16

LOSING AND REGAINING MY WOMANHOOD

I am now more than ever a full woman. But it has not always been so. Thanks to Jo, I gained back what had been stripped from me. I

166

remember the heat in me when young. Even in a dream, I mated with a faceless man, perhaps an anthill; I had my first orgasm. I then knew what the heat of desire was leading to, an experience in which I floated in another planet with a thrilling sensation that I wished could last forever, but it ended fast. The nature of its brevity drove me to desire going through it again and again. Later with Jo in our first night out, I experienced it in a prolonged way. Was Jo the faceless man I had been looking up to for bliss? I would always melt before him even though we avoided the ultimate communion. It took a strong will, but we had managed it since my marriage now in its fifteenth year.

But Nathan took away my sensuality, my desire, and my avid womanhood. Once when I asked him why he would not sleep with me during the day, he asked me back whether I wanted to give birth to an albino child. I pitied him for his beliefs in spite of himself. He did not care about me but for his personal pleasure. He failed to understand that my joy would have redoubled his own joy. I lost my orgasm very early with him, and for so many years turned off my sexual desire with him. He did not help matters by denying me sex for a year and months as a punishment for my purported rebellion against him. He suspected wrongly that I might be gaining sexual pleasure from elsewhere. I communicated with Jo, but he did not stop by in Barkin Ladi or Bukuru apart from once before this time. And then too, we did not go to every length though the opportunity was there. I now throw away any barriers from my emotional life and expect Jo to give me all the pleasure that I have for so long been denied.

I had cherished my body through my student days. My skin glowed no matter what type of pomade or cream I rubbed. It was like boiled palm oil, a complexion many ladies envied. When I took my bath, I cleaned myself with a sponge and ran my fingers over my parts—they tingled at my own touch. My breasts remained erect up to this day, even after delivering twice. I thank God for my body that Jo would describe as angelic, a divine masterpiece that possesses him.

For a long time my body remained unresponsive. I felt no arousal at home. I felt if I had been a whore, the unfeeling sexuality would have saved me through the profession. If my husband felt that since he paid a bride price on me, he had a right to abuse me and yet have me, he treated me worse than a whore should even be treated—he was getting his money's worth. Worse than a whore because he still treated me as a slave upon that—cook, bed-maker, provider, and object of harassment, as he wished. Bless my two boys that removed me from regretting it all. I resisted with every fiber of my heart his intrusion and abuse of my sovereign body. I am not the sort that you will rob and enjoy. Whatever you rob from me will give you a cold metallic taste, an experience that will make you regret the robbery itself. I deliberately made what he took from me without my consent or cooperation sour to taste. I suspect he must have blamed himself afterwards whenever he felt he conquered me despite my resistance. That man could attempt to make love with a corpse! I have been two women in one all along. As a housewife, my flesh was cold; but as Jo's friend, my body tingled with excitement with thoughts or touch of him. Thinking of him flushed me with passionate feelings and put me on heat. Many times I was alone in bed and imagining his caressing me everywhere he wished and that fantasy aroused me to have an orgasm. That was always when I was alone at home. I did not want the presence of the patriarch to sour the daydream that sustained my life.

It happened more often after he wrote me or I wrote him. His words were so tender that they touched me where I would be aroused the most. My breasts stood up and I was wet within with excitement, as I read his letters or poems that made me thrice a lady. Whenever I wrote him too, I experienced the same orgasmic feelings. There were times I should have shouted in excitement and did not care who heard me when I was high in the clouds of fantasy. Maybe I was destined to be a lover, a mistress if you term it so, of an artist rather than the wife of a frigid and self-doubting professional. I enjoyed myself as a lover, but hated myself as a wife. I wish those roles were reversed, but I have decided to live the reality of these contradictions.

So when he intimated long ago that he would visit, I exploded emotionally inside with excitement. "Come, I am ready for you," I wrote back like one possessed. I knew that even if I had to be caught with him and be publicly humiliated, our meeting this time would be more than worth anything else in our lives. I knew my daydream would come true in July, five weeks away.

The reminiscences were part of the communion that lit our faces and hearts. The heart bubbled with excitement. There was so much to share in the past, the present, and the future. How we would share the future, we could not tell yet, but somehow we felt destined to be together even if we were restrained in separate prison houses that we now called our homes.

Reminiscences of days when we drank wine that had not fermented but later did so in our hearts—it drove us literally crazy. How else would you describe Mubi when for two days we were ensconced in a love nest? A love nest, it definitely was. Time and place contracted into one unbroken moment of just being together and talking with each other—one issue led to another, and to another, until we discovered that night and day had become one session of unblinking love. Mubi remains indelibly imprinted in our minds and souls.

So were the days that shuttled us to Bagauda and delivered us at the end of each day at the University Hotel. A life of adventures in which we could have crashed in a night storm in Kano had bound us together. Now we relive the past in this plateau of munificence. I have been raised to a mountain from the valleys of despondence. I am vibrant, sunsplashed. I have regained my real body that had been robbed from me by a mismatch that remains the enigma of my life. My body is now truly a sovereign

169

state. Now let the winds blow! Let the earth shake! Let there be light or darkness! I am transported beyond measure, propelled beyond any previous heights I had attained.

Here's the beloved one who knows me so well, who knows what tenderness does for a partner, the many wars it can win over brute force. I have told him to have his fill of me, as I will have of him. This coalescing of happy moments remembered, expected, and lived cancel out all the years of torture. The scars of old bruises remain, but my favorite has removed the pains with his love and I am healed in this magic touch. Even if customs and our spouses robbed from us many things that we could share together, the most cherished—love—could not. We kept that always safe from intrusion, safe for the other whenever and wherever we met. You can understand the love feast that denial has incensed in us. The more of the communion, the more we wanted for our salvation from the tyranny of patriarchs and matriarchs. We wanted freedom from all forms of tyranny.

Part IV: Others

17

AFTER AN ETERNITY

Jo Ogbe came to spend a week in Bukuru. Apart from the time spent in the hotel, he toured the rocky city. He went to the tin mines, where for about sixty years the earth continued to be disemboweled for plunder of the wealth within. His old friend, William Efe, had obeyed the call for a much higher salary in the oil industry and left for Shell in Port Harcourt. Life in the mines had its own routine, its jargon that was esoteric to the stranger he was. The tin mines brought fame to this city, which had contributed to the national wealth. Long before petroleum was discovered in the southern part of the country, tin, manganese and cobalt from the Bukuru area enriched the colonial administration and later the newly independent nation. The small entrepreneurs who then pursued the challenge of a clear source of wealth by digging the earth for the hidden treasures had now become big companies worth hundreds of billions of naira.

The mines though were suffering a decline in production. At a time miners and anthropologists competed for who could dig the deepest and widest in the area. The anthropologists excavated many terra cotta figures that became world famous as Nok. Miners, caring more for their tin, sold whatever artifacts they found to the anthropologists, art historians, and dealers, who invaded the place for their own reasons. The workers were no longer as many as in the heydays of the tin rush. The price in the world market had fallen to an all-time-low, and only die-hard miners who had nothing else fulfilling to do remained. What a change!

Nearby small towns and villages have always had their tales of woe. The colonialists came and saw the rare mineral and wanted to create a Rand in Plateau Province. They destroyed the local tin smelting to ensure the growth of European companies. The British granted the mining companies a free-range "mining lease" over lands of local people, community land that had been farmed from the beginning of time. With the heavy earth-moving equipment, the companies devastated large areas of the land. With outcries from the people, the companies were forced to pay compensations for land. However, the so-called compensations were more of a public relations drive than a real effort to help the poor peasants—they were a mere token gesture to legitimize outright land seizure. The clever colonialists imposed taxes, which they raised frequently to force people to work for money in the mines, rather than in their farms. There was deforestation with the cutting down of trees for houses and firewood to cater for the needs of the mineworkers. Bukuru and Barkin Ladi had started as mining camps.

Though Jo had last visited Bukuru two years ago, he did not leave the University Guest House where he stayed to moderate the examination papers. It was when he came to see Annie before her marriage sixteen years ago that he really toured the town.

This time, he was here on his own to see Annie. He remembered and returned to some of the places he had always loved. He went to the zoo and museum. He was disappointed at the changes, which had taken place. The museum in which he had seen the largest collection of pottery in Africa was virtually closed. A sign was posted at the door of the exhibition section: CLOSED FOR REPAIRS. The administrative side was full of workers without any work to do. At least, that was what it seemed to him.

The zoo and the museum shared the same large space that was fenced round. He bought his ticket and entered the zoo. It was like an abandoned place. There were no guides. Nor could he see any worker tending to the animals that were supposed to be there. Almost every enclosure or cage had the name of the animal that was supposed to be there. He peeped in, but there was no animal in sight. He saw a worker from afar and beckoned on him to come to him. He, in fact, walked towards him.

"Where is the lion that is supposed to be here?" he asked.

"It died last week," he replied.

"What killed it?" Dr. Ogbe asked.

"I don't know. All the animals just de die like that-o," he said.

Pressed, the worker admitted that the lion was starved to death. The few animals that still had life in them had become wraiths; all had emaciated and could barely move. He learnt that the workers, who had not been paid for almost a year, took for their own upkeep the money they were supposed to use to buy food for the animals. It was a choice they had to make, he explained, or they themselves and their families would starve to death. Why throw a chicken to a crocodile or a goat to a lion when people are starving? Much of the zoo was overgrown with weed, and Dr. Ogbe nearly stepped upon a python, which might have escaped its enclosure or came from outside the zoo.

It was only the art building outside the zoo that Dr. Ogbe saw things to cheer about. There were sculptures and paintings, blending traditional and modern styles. The same piece displayed abstract and naturalistic qualities all in one. The paintings of an artist who worked in the museum were on display and for sale at moderate prices. He purchased an abstract work that he wanted to present to Annie.

Jo's visit this time was different from the other times he and Annie had come together. Though Annie warned months earlier that he should be careful during his visit, they went together to many places. She had come from Barkin Ladi to Bukuru to see him every day. They went to several restaurants and almost behaved as spouses in their hometowns. Annie took the opportunity of Dr. Nathan Goomsay's daily presence at the Club every night to spend as much of her time as she wished with Jo. After all, The State Polytechnic was on vacation. The children's secondary schools were still in session and so she had so much time to herself. For some change of

173

heart, she felt the burden of marital responsibility, which had hung around her like an albatross, had dropped. She felt light and relieved in a state of feeling that she felt strange but welcome. In the meeting two years ago, she had acted as if stalked by a jealous man. This time she behaved as if she did not care about the jealous man but about herself and the man she loved. She did not care whether those who knew her husband saw her with another man—that was their problem, not hers, she told herself. People came from Barkin Ladi to Bukuru for shopping of sophisticated items. It had more to offer in many ways. Here, Annie and Jo even held hands at the Zongo Dutse Park outside the town.

They mutually read each other's heart as having had enough of keeping up appearances to uphold the demands of their roles as wife and husband of different people.

"The time has come for me to choose one of my two men," Annie told Jo.

"It's time for me too to choose one of my two women," he replied. "Why do you have to do yours now like me?"

"I should ask you that question," Jo replied.

That night Annie got home after midnight, though still before Nathan returned from the club. She expected him to be home earlier so as to start a fight, and she was ready to tell him that she had had enough of him. She fell asleep before the man came back to his cold meal on the table.

The week in Bukuru passed so fast for Jo Ogbe. Annie had to take him to the airport to catch the flight to Lagos. She had left without telling the snoring Nathan where she was going. She had made up her mind to accompany Jo to the airport. The long drive to the airport gave them an opportunity to talk more about the future. What they had talked about earlier started to become clear. Annie had suggested that she would transfer to the new State University about to be established, and, if not possible, resign from her position in Barkin Ladi and go to the National University in Abuja. Now she wanted to take up the offer of accommodation from the Governor and live on her own terms. That would start the physical separation that she expected would lead to divorce and her being independent. Once she did that, Dr. Ogbe would transfer to the new university or Abuja after his tenure as Deputy Vice Chancellor, one year of two had gone. With this plan they could both be in the same State University. In the worst scenario, one could be in Abuja and the other nearby where the new State University would be sited. From all indications, it would probably be at Bukuru or Fiala. Since there was already a federal university in Bukuru, Fiala stood a better chance. She and her committee had recommended a place that would open up with the new institution.

Jo and Annie would work out the details, but all at once everything denied them in the past appeared possible. They would through letters fine-tune the arrangements, which could take several years but which they strongly believed would work out well for both of them. How Jo would leave Maria, he had not thought out precisely. But they had decided to separate themselves from their custom-dictated roles and exercise their rights to live, as they liked to.

Annie saw quite a few people who knew her and her husband, greeted them, and followed Dr. Ogbe onto the waiting lounge. All travelers in the whole of Plateau State used the same airport. Nobody bothered her with questions of how her husband fared. She and Jo walked and talked with such a confident air that would have eliminated any form of suspicion of infidelity before those who knew her. She had become a well-known woman in the State anyway and she received official visitors. She waited for passengers to be called to board the plane before leaving. She wanted to spend as much time as available with Jo before he left. They took a seat and chatted as they waited for the call for the Lagosbound flight. The lounge was a little crowded, and everybody seemed to be absorbed in his or her own company. Dr. Ogbe asked her what she would drink and went for two bottles of water. Bukuru was the home of spring

175

water—it was one of its major industries, next to Rock beer and Nabisco crackers. They seeped their water as they discussed the major issue of the day, the military leader's effort to contest as the only candidate for the presidential election to usher in civilian rule.

"The military think Nigerians have a very short memory," Annie told him.

"Wait, you'll see. As the Greeks say, those the gods want to destroy they first make mad."   "Certainly," she said.

"After being President for over five years and things have been deteriorating, why can't he allow others to try their hands at solving the problems before us?" he asked.

"That's the problem of rulers. Once there, on the seat of power, the temptation to continue enjoying the privileges of state becomes so irresistible for many and that's why this hyena will die."   "The greedy fly will end up with the corpse in the grave," responded Annie.

"Sure, it will," Jo said.

As they conversed, the call came to board the plane. They got up, shook hands, and looked at each other for a long moment, then embraced. They cared not for any onlookers as they obeyed their feelings.

"Take care of yourself," Dr. Ogbe told her.

"Take care of yourself too," Annie said.

"Bye!"

"Bye!"

And both parted, misty eyed. Some passengers and others looked at them as they reluctantly parted. Annie headed out of the lounge for the parking lot.

18

WHEN FATE SETS AN AMBUSH

It was a Saturday. Annie drove from the airport straight home. As she drove, she reflected on her condition. She wanted respect. Yes, she needed respect. She did not want to be controlled. She had a mind of her own and knew what to do. How men of Nathan's type could think they are more intelligent than any woman puzzled her. She needed to do things, if possible suffer from her errors and learn from them. She also wanted to be treated as a woman. She respected whoever treated her with respect and like a woman should.

Barkin Ladi roads were busy with people going to the main market or taking care of business that the working week did not allow to be done. Young men rolled wheelbarrows of fruits and foodstuffs for sale. Girls carried bowls of groundnuts, garden eggs, or oranges, which they sold along the roads. Men and women sold vegetables. Most of these were left uncovered from the dust raised by passing vehicles. If people's immunity had not been very strong, so many would die every day from these dustladen foodstuffs, Annie told herself. She saw why she needed to wash her foodstuffs thoroughly before cooking. She would rest when she got home and go to the main food market in the late afternoon. Then there would be a bigger press of people, but she needed to rest for some time before setting out for the market. The days of Jo's visit had been physically and emotionally exhausting for her. She wanted to be a good hostess to her friend and now that he had left, she felt weak and needed to recuperate her energy. Foodstuffs were cheaper in the main market than elsewhere in town and she could save quite a bit from good shopping.

Annie had been away from home for about five hours. She had left early after leaving Nathan's breakfast as usual on the table. His food was still on the table as she left it. His being out was not surprising, because in recent times he had been frequenting the Tin Club of which he was the Clerk. His fellow drinkers and drunkards had elected him their Clerk. He had to open and close the club, place order for drinks, and arrange for the *naisuya* and the woman who prepared pepper soup for the day to get things ready before club members began to stream in. Saturday was always busy, day or night. Some members started drinking from late morning. He, as secretary of the club, also paid the workers on weekends. It was like having both an early shift and a late shift at work without pay. Dr. Goomsay drank much. In fact, nobody who did not drink much alcohol had been elected Clerk of the Tin Club since its inception from colonial times. He drank Guinness and came home already knocked out by the alcohol. He loved the blackness of the drink, which was nicknamed "Black Power." Many of its male drinkers boasted it raised the level of their virility, and that spurred Dr. Goomsay to drink only Guinness in the hope that it would bring him what he needed. He had a date with Mary Nuk on Monday, two days away, and he wanted to ensure he disappointed neither her nor himself. As he drank, he bought drinks for others who came from work before visiting the Club.

"I have to promote the state industry," he would say giving Rock beers to others.

"You are a patriot, prince," they addressed him.

He must have told them about the tussle for the chief's position, or they knew him from his hometown. Some of his secondary school mates had come to Barkin Ladi to make a living and they met in the Club. It was strange that none of them was a close friend, and nobody visited him at home.

"You will become Chief of the Tin Kingdom, the Gwom of Kwaton" they encouraged him, after taking his drinks, eyes bloodshot from too much alcohol.

They laughed together, gossiped, and talked about their dalliances. The almost all-male club did not allow married women in. Not that it was the law, but the few women members were unmarried. The men brought their girlfriends when they chose to. Sometimes women met them there. It was there that Dr. Goomsay first met Mary Nuk, who became his regular girlfriend over the years.

Dr. Goomsay had an account, which had been growing. Though Clerk, a paid "boy" wrote down the names of those who bought drinks or food on credit. So, nothing was waived for the Clerk of the Tin Club. In his pages were dates and prices of drinks, fried meat, or pepper soup bought on credit for more than a year. Every day added hundreds of naira to his account.

Dr. Goomsay drank a lot, but in recent months drank even much more and got home very late and tongue-tied. Frequently he vomited—he got fast to the toilet to pour his mess. This night, like most nights since his elevation to Clerk of the Tin Club, he came back late. Annie had gone to the market and prepared dinner, which was covered on the table for him to eat whenever he returned. She had gone to bed a little early, tired from being busy all day. The previous days have also contributed to the fatigue. Dr. Goomsay came in shaking and swaying from one side to another; he could not maintain a firm posture. Though he had his keys, he knocked loudly at the door. Annie at first wondered who could be knocking at the door so loudly at that late hour. She peeped from a side window and saw her husband. He used to be drunk, but he had never banged on the door when he returned. She knew that there was something wrong in the owner of a house having his keys knocking or banging at the door to his own house. She expected there was going to be trouble for her. She was the one always enduring the brunt of his drunkenness. She opened the door, and as she gave him way to enter, he pushed her with force. She staggered backwards and, fortunately for her, did not fall on the floor but on one of the cushion chairs in the sitting room. It was one of the now regular blackout nights. Dr. Goomsay groped his way to the kitchen, as if that was the dining section. At first he was blinded by the thick darkness from seeing. However, the place became lighter, but blurred. He used his hands to brush the kitchen table but there appeared to be nothing there that he wanted. He went to the adjacent sink, where his hands came upon some plates. He seized the plates and threw them on the floor.

"You witch, don't give me your food again," he shouted.

This was a violent spell of a different kind that she had not experienced before.

"You think I don't know that you are the cause of all my problems. Damn you," he yelled.

Annie lay in the chair, quiet. She had learnt not to answer him, but more than ever, what he said now did not deserve an answer. She watched him from close range, neither afraid nor amused. He fell down on the floor, rather slumped, and began to vomit on his clothes. He fell asleep in that stinking state on the floor, snoring loud.

As soon as she saw that he was asleep, Annie brought the hurricane lamp and cleaned the smelly floor. She also cleaned as much of him that would not disturb his sleep because she wanted him to sleep out the alcohol. She then went to her room and locked herself in. She feared he might have got the gun and could in his drunken delirium be dangerous. There was nothing somebody out of his mind could not do, she surmised. She went to bed and thought of how she was going to rid herself of this succubus of a man. She had borne enough and it was high time she divested herself totally from this drunken man's grip. She had been undecided all along about the marriage because of her children and the hope that things might still work well in the end, but now she had promised Jo it would be over in a short while. She now felt she could adequately take care of the children outside their father's house. Whether they lived with her or not, she would give them her love. But she had to leave this house and live the way she felt she should. Should she walk out on him now, or seize the opportunity of the next quarrel that he would surely start to leave? She no longer cared for what her uncle would say. Justice Solomon Obida had on a brief stop at their home recently asked them to be more cheerful and loving as a couple. He had stopped by to congratulate his niece on her appointment as the Executive Secretary of State University Establishment Committee. Both Annie and Nathan then

180

knew that he might have heard of their cold relationship, but none volunteered the details of their marriage woes to him. Men had a way of absolving other men from their irresponsibility. She fell asleep in the midst of her thoughts of how to execute her separation.

Dr. Goomsay woke about six o'clock with a thunderous shout that would have woken many people in the neighborhood.

"You are not going to work today. You have to keep me company at home. Let us make all the love we have not been making all these months," he said with a laugh that was half a sneer and the other half a joke.

He had forgotten that it was Sunday. Drink could really rob a man of his mind, Annie thought in her room.

He pushed his way to the bedroom, hoping to find Annie in bed. He did not know that she slept in her separate room.

"If you want to sleep with someone outside, I'll kill you. I'll carve out your vagina and feed your lover with it," he shouted.

"Mommy is in her room," Celia told him.

"Is she hiding from me?" he shouted.

Celia saw danger in his eyes and ran outside. She could tell that in those bloodshot eyes and smelly clothes lurked a potential murderer. She had feared the man ever since he played the weird game with her on his lap.

Before he could drag himself to Annie's door, he tripped and fell. He cursed loudly, holding to his leg that started to bleed. Annie had opened her door and left the room. He stood by the door, carrying a club and knocking about the wall and doors with it.

Annie let out a wailing cry that pierced the early morning air that was heavy with fog. The wail brought out many of the residents nearby out of their homes. They instinctively knew that there must be an emergency for that type of sorrowful wail. Neighbors had to respond to each other's problem and help in such cases. The men among them ventured out and saw Annie wearing a sleeping gown with a wrapper tied over it. They were used to fracas in the Goomsay household, but altercations had always been at night. The marital quarrel that endured till morning must be a difficult one, many thought. But it was their responsibility to answer their neighbor's call, and they did.

Dr. Goomsay had gone outside in his soiled and smelling clothes. He waved the club round his head like a child playing a game. He was suddenly quiet and stared at people as if he did not know them as his neighbors. He started a weird dance that convinced the onlookers that the man was out of his mind.

"He came home late last night drunk," Annie told those gathered around.

"Alcohol doesn't survive sleep with this strength," somebody said.

"Madam, this is beyond your power," they told her.

As Dr. Goomsay wanted to leave the front of the house for somewhere, the men felt they had to stop him. They could not allow him in this sorry state to go into the street. Many shook their heads, suspecting what none wanted to say out. None of them was ready to name his sickness. The men sprang on him from all sides and held him down. Breathing fast and heavily, he shouted for his gun.

"Why are the police still holding the gun I have paid for?" he asked the bewildered people holding him.

He had become a violent and therefore dangerous animal who had to be subdued with caution by several men. He seemed to possess a secret physical power that nobody had associated with him. He attempted to forcefully release himself, but could not get off the grip of the many men holding him down.

He ended up that morning in Barkin Ladi Specialist Hospital, where doctors knew him and were shocked. After all, some saw him only the previous night at the club drinking and giving out drinks with left and right to whoever cared to drink the Rock beer he did not drink himself. The attendant nurses wheeled him to a bed, a private room for important patients. Dr. Rajan Gupta, an Indian doctor of immense experience, took charge of his case. Most of the doctors in the dilapidated hospital were expatriates from the Indian sub-continent. They had remained in their jobs even when the poor national economy had diminished any advantage of working in a foreign country. They saved nothing from their salaries to repatriate home. Most of their Nigerian counterparts had left to seek money wherever available. Some left to serve military rulers, join political parties in the hope of party or political jobs when soldiers handed over power to civilians. Others became contractors of general supplies. Many also left for Saudi Arabia or the United States to make thousands of dollars from the high-paying profession.

Dr. Rajan Gupta was a member of the Tin Club but did not take alcohol and so was not a beneficiary of Dr. Goomsay's nightly generosity. He was a vegetarian and so did not take *suya*, the popular spiced roasted meat. He also did not try pepper soup. He sipped his Fanta gently until he wanted to leave. He often engaged in conversations with his colleagues, but he appeared very private. He took time off in his hospital office to meditate. Once in a while he felt Nigerian professionals were too lax morally, but he was not the sort to pass judgement on others. To him, every human being should take to his or her choice of path. He was content with his way of life, to which he would not attempt to convert others. He felt that other people were enjoying their choices; hence they persisted in them. Lean and tall, he looked very athletic and had not changed much in appearance in the twenty years he had been at this hospital.

Dr. Gupta knew a bad case when he saw one and Dr. Nathan Goomsay's was such. He was neither a psychiatrist nor a psychologist, but he knew that his patient's case was deeper than met the eye. He would tranquilize him and observe his behavior after waking. Then he would make his recommendations. He had observed with dismay the increase in psychiatric cases among Nigeria's middle class and was at a loss to understand why. If the very poor in the society could maintain their sanity, what stopped those who preyed on them from doing the same? he asked himself. He had been in the country for the past twenty-one years, one year in Kaduna and the other years in Barkin Ladi, and was as informed as any Nigerian intellectual on the national debacle.

Dr. Gupta prescribed sedatives for his hyperactive patient, who fell asleep immediately. By this time Annie had come to the hospital after driving to inform the older Goomsay about his brother who was flipping over the edge.

"But I saw him yesterday afternoon and he was quite hale and hearty," he said.

"I don't know what happened to him, but he came home very late drunk and collapsed on the floor to sleep as soon as I opened the door for him," Annie told him. "We have never had a history of this sort of thing in our family. What is the world coming to with these strange happenings? Are you telling me a Goomsay is out of his mind?" her brother-in-law asked.

Annie kept quiet, subdued. She was shattered emotionally. Within her, she was asking why this should be happening at this time. Only yesterday she was devising ways of separating, now she had to take care of one with whom she had been yoked for so many years. But now was not the time to condemn Nathan but to help in every possible way to bring him to normalcy. She wanted to make her children proud of their father. The unpleasant experience of the past should not stop her from caring for him for now.

"There's no time to waste. I'll follow you immediately to the hospital and let's see what can be done to calm him," the older Goomsay said.

He went into his bedroom to take wads of naira notes, and came out to jump into the car for the hospital. Both hurried to the men's ward, where a nurse directed them to Dr. Goomsay's room. They saw him asleep but still creased with tension. Mr. Barnabas Goomsay asked to see the doctor treating his brother.

Dr. Rajan Gupta came after attending to another emergency case. He invited both Annie and Mr. Goomsay to his office to discuss with them the condition of his patient.

"You must be Mrs. Goomsay. I have seen the face before. Your husband needs special care," Dr. Gupta told Annie.

"He's my husband's senior brother," Annie said, introducing her brother-in-law to the doctor.

"Sorry, Mr. Goomsay, the case appears very critical. Both of you are the closest to him, apart from his children, I suppose, and you have to make up your minds as soon as possible on what line of treatment you will accept. He will need psychiatric treatment, and you know the good mental asylum is in Kano, and not here in Barkin Ladi. He may have to be transferred there as soon as possible."

Mr. Goomsay closed his eyes, in prayer or mere reflection, for a few moments. He appeared holding down tears. Annie looked at the ground with her eyes already wet. She thought of the creature in famine holding to its teeth a dead fly, which it could not eat and yet would not throw away. She was that creature now.

"Doctor," Mr. Goomsay said, "I will prefer my brother to be treated at home. Let's observe him when he gets over this and see whether it was the drinks or something else wrong with him. There is no history of insanity in my family and it will be too much for the family to bear."

"Health histories are being created daily. New sicknesses break out where they are not expected. In any case, we could transfer him to another ward, but in the end he has to be taken to specialists in Kano if his case remains psychiatric," the doctor told wife and brother of the patient.

Mr. Goomsay, thinking more of the shameful implications than the health problem itself, still argued for observation. He would make sure that his brother stopped drinking. He would advise him to get back to

185

work rather than be idle and under financial pressure. For some months, he had been giving him pocket money to buy basic things he could not ask Annie money for. "He will be a dangerous case if you choose to keep him at home.

I'll prescribe some medications, which he should take daily to relax him. His problem will return when he is under stress. And so many things can trigger a relapse. It is like combustible material waiting to be inflamed. Just be very careful."

Annie and Mr. Goomsay were able to persuade the doctor for Nathan to stay in his current room while he received treatment. A private room in the hospital curtailed visitors streaming in. Annie had to go back and forth, preparing food and bringing it to him to eat. Though sleeping most of the time and drowsy, he ate voraciously. His eating gave the doctor hope that he had come out of the woods of insanity for the time being.

A week after he was bound and taken to the hospital, Dr. Goomsay came home. He was quiet and subdued. He had to take his medication twice a day at breakfast and at dinner. Annie made sure that he took them though they made him drowsy and unsteady when moving in the house. However, he had to take them. He behaved like a child, always expecting attention from Annie and Celia.

Annie had more than enough chores now to occupy her entire day. But she still had to go to the office to attend to matters relating to her committee and quickly run home to be on guard lest the combustible one in the house set himself, somebody else, or the entire house ablaze. Once the Commissioner of Education summoned her to the Ministry for a discussion, which sounded more like a job interview than anything else. She was asked to submit her curriculum vitae and her tax clearance certificate. She complied with the requests. She wouldn't mind transferring to the new State University as Associate Professor or Professor. That would fit her plan to leave Barkin Ladi to wherever she would be outside Nathan's house. Nobody knew the heavy heart she carried.

At home Annie was scared and wanted to discuss with Nathan's brother to see a psychiatrist in Kano, as recommended by Dr. Gupta. She lived with the problem and, from Nathan's complaints of sleeplessness at night, feared the problem could flare up again and soon. She was sitting on a time bomb and only she knew the extreme situation. Nathan's brother was bent on sweeping the problem under the carpet, as if that would cure his brother. Meanwhile, Annie pondered over her own condition, especially what fate had inflicted on her at the moment of not just nearing a decision but also implementing it.

Annie wrote Jo about the situation in which she found herself. The children were home on vacation, the patriarch sedated all day to keep him from flipping over little things, and she had to go to the office once in a while to check what mails or messages she had. The vacation was getting over soon and how was she going to cope with so many things at the same time?

19

SEEKING SALVATION

From the very beginning, Father Brown was seen as a rising star in the Catholic Mission. It did not take too long before he was elevated to the position of Bishop. Now Bishop Brown, he maintained with a warm heart and keen eyes his bishopric at St. Patrick's Cathedral that stood conspicuously near Warri's Main Market. It was an elevation every member of his congregation expected. He was the only white reverend father left in the diocese, and the African ones did not have a godfather as he had in the retiring bishop, who brought him there from Cork anyway. It was rumored that Bishop Kevin O'Flannagan was very sick and wanted to be sure that his favorite and choice for the position he would vacate was installed before he left or died.

Brown's promotion was not only due to favoritism. In the two decades he had been the officiating priest in the largest church in the diocese, he had learnt to speak as fluently as a European could possibly do the three major languages of his congregation: Urhobo, Itsekiri, and Izon. Of course, he spoke each of them with a heavy accent. While children laughed at him when he spoke outside the church, adults praised him for his industry. After all, few Nigerians could speak the language of their neighbors. He was also proficient in Pidgin English, which many halfliterate Catholics used at confession.

Bishop Brown had a very good memory. He kept a mental record of the private and public lives of his flock. He had consistently asked Mr. and Mrs. Numa about Maria's whereabouts and condition. Maria's parents had maintained a good relationship with him despite their ban from Holy Communion. He frequently asked them whether their daughter had succeeded in taking her man to the altar for holy matrimony. The Numas had no information of any change in their daughter and son-in-law's remarriage. Of course, that meant that their ban remained. So the Holy Father knew from Maria's parents her move to Lagos, where she taught in a secondary school as her husband taught at the University.

"How is Omose?" the priest would ask Mrs. Numa.

"He is a big boy now. He has just finished his secondary school and about to enter the university," she replied.

"Alleluia!" the priest chanted.

"Praise the Lord," Mrs. Numa added.

"And Titi?" he asked.

"She is fine. She is in a secondary school."

"Alleluia!" he again chanted.

Bishop Brown got the mailing address of the Ogbes from Maria's parents. A few times they had visited Warri from Lagos, Mrs. Numa had asked them to go and see the Catholic cleric, but they declined. She even told the bishop of their visit once, but he had engagements throughout the day and missed the opportunity of surprising the Ogbes. He pursued deviants, as he called those married without the Catholic matrimonial sacrament, till he turned them to the right course.

Maria was very surprised to receive a letter from Bishop Brown. In the one-page handwritten letter, he wielded a stick and a carrot simultaneously. He wrote:

I have constantly asked your parents about you. Mrs. Numa has been very kind in telling me about your condition and your husband's career. She gave me your address. I hope you and your family are fine. The Lord will always take care of you. But you must always have the Lord in your mind and never forget to pray daily and worship him on Sundays.

How is Omose? I understand he is grown up and getting ready to enter the university. How is Titi, my little girl of those days? How time flies! Glory to Jesus! Honor to Mary! Alleluia! I understand that you are

doing well and I hope that since you live among people of different faiths, including Muslims, you don't forget your own Catholic faith. Maria, how long will you continue to live in sin? Life is short, and you have to make peace with Christ before it is too late. Death is a thief and it comes unannounced. You have to save your soul. What does it profit a man to have all the riches of the world and lose his own soul? So, there is no way you can be all right if you have not consecrated your matrimonial relationship with Jonah Ogbe.
I wait for your reply.

Bishop Patrick Brown.

Unknown to her parents, Maria had joined a Pentecostal Church in Lagos. At the beginning she attended the two churches, St. Andrew's Catholic Church in Yaba and Bible Church of Salvation in the Akoka area of Yaba, as if keeping two obligations. Then she abandoned the Catholic Church, which excluded her from Holy Communion to be a full participant in the services of the new church. This church did not judge you as unworthy, but left you to dialogue with God in your own heart. The charismatic pastor knew that among his congregation were men with two wives, adulterous men and women, fornicators, armed robbers, and other sinners. But he felt it was not his duty to judge them. They would be saved according to the degree of their faith and the state of their lives at the moment of death. He wanted sinners to flock his church and it was left for them to respond to God the way they wanted. After all, many saints were great sinners before their conversion. St. Paul easily came to his mind. Pastor Odekunle preached with the power of the Holy Spirit and his congregation made him happy with their tithes, offerings, and frequent thanksgiving gestures.

Mrs. Maria Ogbe did not miss the all-night service of the last Friday of the month, in which they prayed, sang, and the pastor allowed members of his congregation to freely range in their testimonies. He was as much after their lives as after their souls. He tolerated wealth and did not harp on the poor being blessed. Maria loved the testimonies, many serious and others looking more like fiction than fact. She gave a tenth of her earnings, as the pastor demanded of everybody. She went beyond the pastor's tolerance in her ascetic life. She stripped herself of unnecessary adornments to be pure before God. Big earrings, painted eyelashes and lips, seductive hairdos were devices of the devil to lead astray, according to Pastor Odekunle. Maria had stopped wearing any makeup and stripped herself of jewelry. Jo had asked her several times why she had to go to those lengths to please God, but she said this life was mere vanity. She soon started her fasting, dry fasting as she called it, when she took neither water nor food from sunrise to sundown. And she would do this for three months.

"Why can't you just become a Muslim and fast during the Ramadan?" Jo asked.

"I don't want to be a Muslim. I am a Christian and with the power of Jesus, I will always be okay with the fasting."

During her fasting period, Jo kept away from her. There were times she felt Jo came close to tempt her and called him the devil. Jo respected her faith and went on as if he lived alone. Maria lived normally despite stripping herself of any allurements. She had emaciated though and did not look healthy from the strict fasting.

It first started with a one-day retreat in the church. Then it went to three days, then a week. And soon Maria was traveling to places as far away as Calabar and Kaduna for a week or two for Christian Crusades. Her principal complained about her frequent absences from school and warned he would recommend stopping her salary. Maria began to ask Jo for money to pay for registration for retreats and crusades. She wanted to go to Calabar for one of the many crusades and needed six thousand naira. She would register with two thousand and pay for her accommodation and food with another three or so. And that sum upon her transportation from Lagos to Calabar by bus.

"Don't you think you are making somebody rich at my expense with these crusades?" Jo asked.

"That's not your problem, it is mine," she retorted.

"But it is more my problem if I have to provide you money," Jo responded.

Jo still gave her the money she needed, but knew that he had lost his wife to evangelist crusaders. Maria's sudden religiosity had made a bad case worse. He was not surprised when he returned from his trip to Bukuru, ostensibly to visit the university but in reality to re-connect with Annie, to see that Maria had changed even more. She was excited in an unusual way. She prepared a good dish in anticipation of his return from travel. It was the case of the toad out in daylight, something was happening, which he least guessed.

"I am going to devote myself to Christ," she announced. She made the sign of the cross, which made Jo to suspect she was back to her Catholic beginning.

She had nudged Jo unsuccessfully the past many years for them to go to church and have a priest conduct the sacrament of matrimony. Jo insisted that the traditional marriage was legal and binding enough and that he was not going to bow to white people's culture to placate her fears of going to hell. She had recently warned him that if he failed to do the right thing, as she put it, she would leave him and cleanse herself of any sinful taint. Jo felt she was just bluffing.

"I am going to a theology school at Ibadan to learn to become a pastor. I want to start my own church in Warri, and I will have to leave you and Lagos. Omose is grown up and is in the university. Titi is also big enough to follow me or stay with you. Both of them will understand my decision," she concluded.

Jo covered his eyes with his two palms, took a deep breath and exhaled. He was at a loss on what to say to a woman who wanted to save her soul.

"Do what pleases you and your lord."

"My lord is also your lord. Praise be to Jesus! Amen," she chanted. Maria replied Bishop Brown soon afterwards. She wrote the Catholic bishop thus:

My salvation is in my hands. I am taking care of my soul, and my life should not be a source of worry to you. I will be going to the Theological College, Ibadan, and will eventually become a pastor of a church I intend to start in Warri. Thanks for your concern, but I am more than you aware of my own spiritual needs. My spouse is now the Holy Spirit, not any human being.

Two days after Maria left Lagos for Ibadan in an apparent separation or divorce, Jo received the letter from Annie regarding the incubus she now had to bear.

20

ON RECORD

Things came to a stage that Mr. Barnabas Goomsay knew that something had to be done urgently. He had to take the advice of Dr. Gupta on seeing a specialist psychiatrist. His brother was showing signs of a major relapse. As he helped in gathering his things before taking him to Kano to see the recommended psychiatrist, he had to open the "safe," the cupboard in which Nathan kept his credentials. Tucked between two books of poems was a sheaf of papers that were clipped to hold together. The papers, letters, and diary entries must have been written at different times the past five years or so. A few were dated but most were not. It appeared the letters had not been mailed and so were not copies but originals.

Dear Magistrate Obida,

I have pondered over reporting your niece, my wife Anna, to you for three years and more. I know whenever you asked about us, I always said we were fine. What else should I say? Even when you stopped by once, I remember we put up appearances though you suspected things were not well with us. Things are far from fine, but I had to lie to cover up the problem that has become a chronic disease. I held back reporting for so long because I didn't want you to dismiss my petition and tell me that I should take care of my domestic problems. You are a man whose daily life hinges on judging right from wrong, so I believe you can help to relieve me in the hell I now find myself.

Has Anna ever reported me to you? I don't think she dares do that because she knows quite well that you will ask probing questions that will embarrass her. If she says I am a bad husband, you might ask her whether she is a good wife. So, she held back from revealing the hell we live in to save her face. I can bear it no longer; hence I am writing you this letter.

She does not listen to me and even ignores that I am around in the house no matter how hard I try to draw her attention. She carries this to the extreme because her mind seems to be somewhere else than this house. All she does is stay at work for as long as possible. She is popular, as you well know, and forgets that she is my wife and not wife of the State. Is it enough for her to be praised at work at my expense? She will say that she leaves food for me, but the food is stale anyway by the time I want to eat it. And is food everything for a man? The food of the mind and soul is more important than the food I can buy in a restaurant or market. I didn't need to marry for that, since I can always eat at the Club.

I don't know why she dresses so well to work to please people I don't know, while she makes no effort to please me at home. I don't know who is in her department or institution to accuse her of having a secret lover there. But she deliberately neglects me and she seems to derive abundant pleasure from doing that to hurt me. There is a limit to which a man can bear his wife's insubordination or misbehavior, after which he reacts in a way that will help him maintain sanity. If it is not Dr. Ogbe, it is her supervisor, head of department, or rector receiving her attention. For sometime now, it is the chairman of her committee. Try to appeal to your niece to be sane with me. For now, she is not sane and is playing with fire.

I feel I should tell you this because you are the person I saw in the family that made me marry her in the first place. I was not keen, unlike my parents who sang her praises to high heaven, on Anna until I knew you were her uncle. A man of distinction like you, though on the maternal side, was an in-law anybody would like to have. It took me years to warm up to the idea despite the engagement ceremony which I didn't participate in anyway. You remember it was in my third year of studies in Edinburgh when I came on vacation that I met you. It was after I met you that I

195

dropped my reservations. It was not her going to the University of Yerwa that impressed me. No, it was you Magistrate Obida who was my role model.

I had misgivings about university education for women, especially those studying the arts reading novels and feeling life is lived as in fiction. I have no time for that. I would have preferred a nurse/midwife, but that is a gone matter.

Please try to call your niece and either you or Madam should tell her what it takes to make a good wife.

Yours sincerely,
Dr. Nathan Goomsay

Dear Justice Obida,
Congratulations on your promotion to a Justice. You very much deserve promotion to the exalted position of Justice of the High Court of Nigeria. I am proud of you. I knew from the beginning that you are going to be on top of your legal profession.

I thought I wrote you two years ago, but found that I did not mail the letter. I hope I will mail this one after writing. I met you twice since then but had no time to tell you anything personal. Social occasions are superficial engagements, everybody tugs you here and there and there is no time for private talks.

The situation in my house is getting from bad to worse. I discovered that Anna is receiving correspondence from one Dr. Jo Ogbe, her former lecturer at the University of Yerwa. He sends poems to her and she writes poems for him. I have intercepted some of their poems but I am yet to get any of their letters. The poems though speak for themselves— they had a relationship, which they don't want to break. How can a married woman be in love with somebody else and will not stop it even when confronted with evidence by her rightful husband?

196

I am thinking of steps to counter her allegiance to another man, who lives far away but has so much control over her. There are women everywhere for any man like me to pick from. She fails to realise that I am a medical doctor and I can have my choice from among so many free women.

She still dresses so beautifully when going out alone or to class. Sometimes it is to her women's association's meetings; at other times it is to her Board meetings or Committee meetings. I don't care where she goes, she is definitely not telling me where she is really going. I don't believe that she has no eye on somebody around too. I am living in hell. Can you imagine what pain to see your own wife going out at will and coming back at anytime she likes and not telling you where she is going most of the time? In recent times she has been more frequent in attending her writers' club and women's organization meetings. Do they write poems together or why should they meet twice a week or even once a week? She has been in these associations for so many years, but all of a sudden they have become a daily preoccupation. I believe these serve as a pretext for her to go out freely. She looks for a quarrel to give her the excuse to turn her back on me. Once she comes back, she hurries to the bathroom and after bathing almost immediately goes to bed. She gets up at odd times to write what I am not allowed to see. I have now devised a way to get into what she is doing. I have a spare key to her bedroom where she hides her secrets. I have found books of poetry sent to her. One is dedicated to her. I will write Dr. Jonah Ogbe to stop corresponding with my wife. Enough is enough. I have been taking lessons in writing poetry and can now write a bit. Maybe this will stop Anna's looking outside. Another poet is now in the house to share her poetry.

I wish that your next promotion be to the Supreme Court of Nigeria. That is where you rightly belong and by the grace of God you will get there.

Yours sincerely,
Dr. Nathan Goomsay

*   *   *

It seems there is a rat eating up things in the house. I have lost some papers, my poems and my recordings of what has been happening in my marital life. This woman may have turned into a rat to eat up every piece of paper I place within reach. She will not see my papers again. I'll lock them up in my cupboard. I am going to put rat poison in the house so that any rat that eats my papers will pay for it dearly. Woe betides her if I should catch her opening my cupboard. She now hides her stuff from me and it takes extreme cunning for me to read her poems and notes. In recent months, I have not discovered new things, though she is still writing. Yet she wants to read my private writings. What is good for the goose should be good for the gander.

*   *   *

I will leave this poem where I think she will see it to read. She will definitely congratulate herself for being an efficient spy, but I know she is a lousy one at that.

It takes two to tangle,
But you want me to tangle alone.
It takes two eyes to see properly, It
takes two ears to hear well,
It takes two legs to walk as a man.
Why did God always make a pair?
To make things function well.

Can you walk or dance on one leg?
Even the witches of Kwaton Have
not achieved that craft! I am a man
you a woman, We two make a
couple. It is nature that binds Two
people into one.
It takes two to tangle,
But you want me to tangle alone.
That's an impossible task.

*   *   *

Dear Dr. Ogbe,

I know that you received my earlier letter to you. It was not a threat but a plea. Things changed for a time in the house. Of recent, I suspect you contacted each other again. I am living with a stranger, whose face I cannot recognize as my wife. If she wrote you first, ignore her. She wants to put you in trouble. Since she knew I placed an order for a double-barreled gun from the police, she has been acting as if she wants to lure you here to be shot. I will not be held responsible for somebody who comes to taunt my manhood before my wife. If you put your hand in the mouth of a shark, you know what will happen to it. Beware.

Yours sincerely,
Dr. Nathan Goomsay

*   *   *

Dear Professor Semshak:

199

Why do you want my wife to be your Executive Secretary? Is that not the same as Private Secretary? You are playing with fire. Leave her alone.

Yours sincerely,
Dr. Nathan Goomsay

*   *   *

She prepared a delicious meal today for me, as she has not done for a very long time. For years I was the last person she thought about before she prepared meals. Maybe she has a change of heart at last. Alleluia! But if she thinks she is going to seduce me with food, she is making a big mistake. She has to listen to me first before I can touch her. I know I am okay now after several years of panic. I will not go close to her yet. She could use her body as a trap to disable me so that she can have a free range with Dr. Ogbe or anybody outside. No way!

*   *   *

If I have to see Mary Nuk outside, I will continue to do so. I go to the Club every night, she tells everybody. Yes, I go to the Club. Once I leave home at night, I go to the Club. Wherever I go at night, it is to the Club. Who is going to tell her at home that I was not at the Club one or two nights a week. I think she thinks she is very smart. I am not smart but know my way around. With Mary Nuk always ready for me, I don't have to take the bluffing at home. When people are about to die of starvation, they won't mind eating poisoned food. That is her business, not mine.

*   *   *

I am not going to write Magistrate, I beg your pardon, Justice Obida again. I am not going to write Dr. Ogbe again. I could not bring myself to mail the Justice's letters. I also left the second letter to her god in the safe. I am not writing the Chairman again. I will take the law into my own

200

hands. I was trained to deal with emergencies. This is an emergency, which I must deal with in my own way.

*   *   *

If she gets the upper hand, how can I walk straight as her husband? She has been made Executive Secretary of the State University Establishment Committee and the papers hail her for the appointment. She is meeting with men in high places and is asked to travel to other universities. She will look for an opportunity to go to Lagos and see Dr. Ogbe and say she is doing her duty. Yes, her duty to him and not to Plateau State! Can I still subdue her to obey my will with this appointment? Events are not helping me at all.

A housewife should be a housewife and not be a public figure. I am sure many men in Barkin Ladi and the Sate are after her and that makes her dress ever more gorgeously than ever. I just hope this appointment doesn't make her head swell. What will become of me if she is appointed the Acting Vice Chancellor? Sometimes we, men, defer to women so that they can pay back in the way we want. How can I stop her from becoming too much of a public figure, which she already is? She appears in The Guardian *and* The Standard *and conducts interviews. First, it was the women's writing club, then the secondary school female drama groups, and the National Organization of Women. Now it is The State University. I have lost control of my wife. I am lost. If she continues to get the upper hand in everything, then I have to take the law into my own hands and treat her as my wife. I have to assert my authority in any way I can. She is my wife, nobody else's wife—she is neither The State Polytechnic's wife, nor Jo Ogbe's or The State University's wife for that matter. Time will tell who has right over her body.*

*   *   *

The trees around are growing so tall, now touching the sky. Everybody around me is growing smaller. The stars are in tears and the sun is blindfolded. Every moving thing seems to be suspended in the air. I cannot stand on my feet—I am so light that slowly, as I want to move, I am swaying in the wind. God, help me. What is happening to me? Is the ruling house in Kwaton after me? May its witchcraft not work on me! I feel well and unwell at the same time. I am heavy and light. I am sane and insane. God, help me. Has this woman's lover asked her to put poison in my food? She has too many lovers now that she is the darling of the State's ministry of education. How did they get to know her? Whom do I hold responsible for my sickness? I am not sick. I have a light head. I will be fine with a dose of Aspirin.

21

THE CRASH

Annie knew she must prepare to accompany Nathan to Kano. She did not know how long they would be there. She had to be with him—he had no sister and nobody else in his family she could think of that would agree to leave work and stay with him. She would go with the brother who would return to his own family as soon as he was admitted into the mental hospital. The scraps of paper from the cupboard that expressed his feelings were moving. Was he just awkward and could not express in action and orally his feelings, or was he really a poor husband? Why, for so many years, were they not able to talk out their problems? Should they have married in the first place? But once married, could she have entombed herself to please him because he wanted her not to relate to anybody else however far away? Could she have done more in all these years to turn him around from an ogre to a complete gentleman? There was no opportunity now to answer these questions.

Annie was in a dilemma over her promise to Jo Ogbe and the fresh impulse to take good care of Nathan. She would go shopping to pick the provisions she needed to sustain them in Kano. She felt it would be better for her to take some things there like cans of milk, beverages, and biscuits than buy from there. She could not trust the hospital to properly feed her husband.

After buying what she needed in the market, she wanted to cheer up Nathan. A card could make him feel more relaxed as a husband than someone threatened. She wanted to be a friendly partner. Once he became well, a few endearments would smooth the rough edges of their relationship. She would make him as happy as she possibly could. She put in so much effort in the relationship a long time ago but fell back when he did not respond perhaps quickly enough. More patience was needed. Jo would understand. After all, he had advised her from the beginning to be a good wife, and it was only when she reported the unbearable state of things that he felt she had to break away. She was trying to break away before the new developments. Should Nathan get well now, they could talk as two people and get the problems between them resolved. So much was going on in her head. She left the market to walk to Ahmadu Bello Road to select a card that would please Nathan and start a new era of amicable relationship. There was no need driving the short distance, more so with the fuel shortage in town. A woman passed with the features of Mary Nuk. Only that she was plumper and looked like a woman in her early pregnancy. She was not sure whether or not she was Mary Nuk, because the woman turned away from her as she tried to look her way. It happened so suddenly as accidents always do. The taxi driver was running from a policeman at a checkpoint on the main street. The driver knew that whether his papers were correct or not, he would still have to give the police money. Of recent, he had not been able to balance daily the fifteen hundred he was supposed to. He either paid the police for no offense or bought fuel at the black market, which consumed his earnings.

He had decided to play hardball with the police. He would not allow any policeman to forcibly extract the little money he made from him. If the policeman wanted, he could pursue him on foot and he would still drive on. He pressed hard on the accelerator to escape. The old Toyota Corolla jerked speedily ahead. Annie was coming directly in front of it and the loud collision drew from others nearby piercing cries. Another accident caused by the police had claimed an innocent life!

It would take several hours to know who had been killed—the prospective acting vice-chancellor of Plateau State University. The State Government Gazette released that morning had published the appointment of Dr. Anna Goomsay the acting vice-chancellor of the newly established Plateau State University to be located at Fiala. She was to run it in her acting capacity for three years before a substantive vice-chancellor would be appointed.

In her bag were sheets of paper that contained poems.

Sovereign Body

I

Calabash in a current I go
towards the sea undeterred
by turbulence— I know I
won't drown but live
excitedly every day of the
journey. I want to enter the
sea, sit upright, moved by
the music of the waves. I
am a calabash, un deterred
by turbulence.

II

*A parrot I kiss a stone— only its
shadow responds, moves
according to light thrown upon it
but not the body of weight I am
bound to day and night in
deference to tradition. Loyalty to
stone hurts deep. On the side, a
palm dances to the music of the
wind, cools my sweating body as
it reels with laughter. What a
life, this limbo! As the sun
wrestles to free itself from
clouds, so I want to break out of
the rock
and live in the oasis of the palm in
the cool breeze of another spot.*

III

*The sunbird relishes the wild open
country where it ranges freely hop
after hop, branch after branch, deep
into the heart of the bush. Its colours
brighten in the sun, its song ripples
loud in the air. After the day's task
comes rest & it goes to its nest of
down to lounge body to body,
ensconced. Spouse or partner, it sings*

a love song sunk in the bosom of the
other. I want to cover myself with his
body, no space between as a cold
divide. I am a sunbird of the wild; the
day advances comes sundown when
abandoned in the nest so shoddily
built but belongs to two.

IV

Already up and cheered on, we must so
quicken our pace in the race to overtake
those ahead of our starting line.

We hold our breaths and through fresh
openings in the tower see far ahead
lazybones of the past in front of hairy chests.

Revolution first ferments in the head before
it possesses the street into action. We shall
overcome distance with our minds.

V

The weather clears after the
apocalyptic storm— in the diary beats
a heart encased in stone now broken.
The long night comes to an end; dawn
in white linen approaches to embrace
two with a smile. I had come close to
dying, entombed— there's no Easter

without Good Friday! The weather
clears after the apocalyptic storm.

Printed in the United States
By Bookmasters